WAR PARTY

WAR PARTY

LOUIS L'AMOUR

BANTAM BOOKS

NEW YORK • TORONTO • LONDON • SYDNEY • AUCKLAND

WAR PARTY
Bantam paperback edition / February 1975
The Louis L'Amour Collection / February 1985

If you would be interested in receiving bookends for
The Louis L'Amour Collection,
please write to this address for information:

The Louis L'Amour Collection
Bantam Books
P.O. Box 956
Hicksville, NY 11801

ISBN 0-553-06271-9

Published simultaneously in the United States and Canada

Bantam Books are published by Bantam Books, a division of
Bantam Doubleday Dell Publishing Group, Inc. Its trade-
mark, consisting of the words "Bantam Books" and the por-
trayal of a rooster, is Registered in U.S. Patent and Trademark
Office and in other countries. Marca Registrada, Bantam
Books, 666 Fifth Avenue, New York, New York 10103.

PRINTED IN THE UNITED STATES OF AMERICA

10   9   8   7   6   5   4   3   2

WAR PARTY

TRAP OF GOLD

Wetherton had been three months out of Horsehead before he found his first color. At first it was a few scattered grains taken from the base of an alluvial fan where millions of tons of sand and silt had washed down from a chain of rugged peaks; yet the gold was ragged under the magnifying glass.

Gold that has carried any distance becomes worn and polished by the abrasive action of the accompanying rocks and sand, so this could not have been carried far. With caution born of harsh experience he seated himself and lighted his pipe, yet excitement was strong within him.

A contemplative man by nature, experience had taught him how a man may be deluded by hope, yet all his instincts told him the source of the gold was somewhere on the mountain above. It could have come down the wash that skirted the base of the mountain, but the ragged condition of the gold made that improbable.

The base of the fan was a half-mile across and hundreds of feet thick, built of silt and sand washed down by centuries of erosion among the higher peaks. The point of the wide V of the fan lay between two towering upthrusts of granite, but from where Wetherton sat he could see that the actual source of the fan lay much higher.

Wetherton made camp near a tiny spring west of the fan, then picketed his burros and began his climb. When he was well over two thousand feet higher he stopped, resting again, and while resting he dry-panned some of the silt. Surprisingly, there were more than a few grains of gold even in that first pan, so he continued his climb, and passed at last between the towering portals of the granite columns.

Above this natural gate were three smaller alluvial fans that joined at the gate to pour into the greater fan below. Dry-panning two of these brought no results, but the third, even by the relatively poor method of dry-panning, showed a dozen colors, all of good size.

The head of this fan lay in a gigantic crack in a granitic upthrust that resembled a fantastic ruin. Pausing to catch his breath, his gaze wandered along the base of this upthrust, and right before him the crumbling granite was slashed with a vein of quartz that was literally laced with gold!

Struggling nearer through the loose sand, his heart pounding more from excitement than from altitude and exertion, he came to an abrupt stop. The band of quartz was six feet wide and that six feet was cobwebbed with gold.

It was unbelievable, but here it was.

Yet even in this moment of success, something about the beetling cliff stopped him from going forward. His innate caution took hold and he drew back to examine it at greater length. Wary of what he saw, he circled the batholith and then climbed to the ridge behind it from which he could look down upon the roof. What he saw from there left him dry-mouthed and jittery.

The granitic upthrust was obviously a part of a much older range, one that had weathered and worn, suffered from shock and twisting until finally this tower of granite had been violently upthrust, leaving it standing, a shaky ruin among younger and sturdier peaks. In the process the rock had been shattered and riven by mighty forces until it had become a miner's horror. Wetherton stared, fascinated by the prospect. With enormous wealth here for the taking, every ounce must be taken at the risk of life.

One stick of powder might bring the whole crumbling mass down in a heap, and it loomed all of three hundred feet above its base in the fan. The roof of the batholith was riven with gigantic cracks, literally seamed with breaks like the wall of an ancient building that has remained standing after heavy bombing. Walking back to the base of the tower, Wetherton found he could actually break loose chunks of the quartz with his fingers.

The vein itself lay on the downhill side and at the very base. The outer wall of the upthrust was sharply tilted so that a man working at the vein would be cutting his way into the very foundations of the tower, and any single blow of the pick might bring the whole mass down upon him. Furthermore, if the rock did fall, the vein would be hopelessly buried under thousands of tons of rock and lost without the expenditure of much more capital than he could command. And at this moment Wetherton's total of money in hand amounted to slightly less than forty dollars.

Thirty yards from the face he seated himself upon the sand and filled his pipe once more. A man might take tons out of there without trouble, and yet it might collapse at the first blow. Yet he knew he had no choice. He needed money and it lay here before him. Even if he were at first successful there were two things he must avoid. The first was tolerance of danger that might bring carelessness; the second, that urge to go back for that "little bit more" that could kill him.

It was well into the afternoon and he had not eaten, yet he was not hungry. He circled the batholith, studying it from every angle only to reach the conclusion that his first estimate had been correct. The only way to get at the gold was to go into the very shadow of the leaning wall and attack it at its base, digging it out by main strength. From where he stood it seemed ridiculous that a mere man with a pick could topple that mass of rock, yet he knew how delicate such a balance could be.

The tower was situated on what might be described as the military crest of the ridge, and the alluvial fan sloped steeply away from its lower side, steeper than a steep stairway. The top of the leaning wall overshadowed the top of the fan, and if it started to crumble and a man had warning, he might run to the north with a bare chance of escape. The soft sand in which he must run would be an impediment, but that could be alleviated by making a walk from flat rocks sunken into the sand.

It was dusk when he returned to his camp. Deliberately, he had not permitted himself to begin work, not by so much as a sample. He must be deliberate in all his actions, and never for a second should he forget the mass that towered above him. A split second of hesitation when the crash came—and he accepted it as inevitable—would mean burial under tons of crumbled rock.

The following morning he picketed his burros on a small meadow near the spring, cleaned the spring itself and prepared a lunch. Then he removed his shirt, drew on a pair of gloves and walked to the face of the cliff. Yet even then he did not begin, knowing that upon this habit of care and deliberation might depend not only his success in the venture, but life itself. He gathered flat stones and began building his walk. "When you start moving," he told himself, "you'll have to be fast."

Finally, and with infinite care, he began tapping at the quartz, enlarging cracks with the pick, removing fragments, then prying loose whole chunks. He did not swing the pick, but used it as a lever. The quartz was rotten, and a man might obtain a considerable amount by this method of picking or even pulling with the hands. When he had a sack filled with the richest quartz he carried it over his path to a safe place beyond the shadow of the tower. Returning, he tamped a few more flat rocks into his path, and began on the second sack. He worked with greater care than was, perhaps, essential. He was not and had never been a gambling man.

In the present operation he was taking a careful calculated risk in which every eventuality had been weighed and judged. He needed the money and he intended to have it; he had a good idea of his chances of success, but knew that his gravest danger was to become too greedy, too much engrossed in his task.

Dragging the two sacks down the hill he found a flat block of stone and with a single jack proceeded to break up the quartz. It was a slow and hard job but he had no better means of extracting the gold. After breaking or crushing the quartz much of the gold could be separated by a knife blade, for it was amazingly concentrated. With water from the spring Wetherton panned the remainder until it was too dark to see.

Out of his blankets by daybreak he ate breakfast and completed the extraction of the gold. At a rough estimate his first day's work would run to four hundred dollars. He made a cache for the gold sack and took the now empty ore sacks and climbed back to the tower.

The air was clear and fresh, the sun warm after the chill of night, and he liked the feel of the pick in his hands.

Laura and Tommy awaited him back in Horsehead, and if he was killed here, there was small chance they would ever know what had become of him. But he did not intend to be killed. The gold he was extracting from this rock was for them, and not for himself.

It would mean an easier life in a larger town, a home of their own and the things to make the home a woman desires, and it meant an education for Tommy. For himself, all he needed was the thought of that home to return to, his wife and son—and the desert itself. And one was as necessary to him as the other.

The desert would be the death of him. He had been told that many times, and did not need to be told, for few men knew the desert as he did. The desert was to him what an orchestra is to a fine conductor, what the human body is to a surgeon. It was his work, his life, and the thing he knew best. He always smiled when he looked first into the desert as he started a new trip. Would this be it?

The morning drew on and he continued to work with an even-paced swing of the pick, a careful filling of the sack. The gold showed bright and beautiful in the crystalline quartz which was so much more beautiful than the gold itself. From time to time as the morning drew on, he paused to rest and to breathe deeply of the fresh, clear air. Deliberately, he refused to hurry.

For nineteen days he worked tirelessly, eight hours a day at first, then lessening his hours to seven, and then to six. Wetherton did not explain to himself why he did this, but he realized it was becoming increasingly difficult to stay on the job. Again and again he would walk away from the rock face on one excuse or another, and each time he would begin to feel his scalp prickle, his steps grow quicker, and each time he returned more reluctantly.

Three times, beginning on the thirteenth, again on the seventeenth and finally on the nineteenth day, he heard movement within the tower. Whether that whispering in the rock was normal he did not know. Such a natural movement might have been going on for centuries. He only knew that it happened now, and each time it happened a cold chill went along his spine.

His work had cut a deep notch at the base of the tower, such a notch as a man might make in felling a tree, but wider and deeper. The sacks of gold, too, were increasing. They now numbered seven, and their total would, he believed, amount to more than five thousand dollars—probably nearer to six thousand. As he cut deeper into the rock the vein was growing richer.

He worked on his knees now. The vein had slanted downward as he cut into the base of the tower and he was all of nine feet into the rock with the great mass of it above him. If that rock gave way while he was working he would be crushed in an instant with no chance of escape. Nevertheless, he continued.

The change in the rock tower was not the only change, for he had lost weight and he no longer slept well. On the night of the twentieth day he decided he had six thousand dollars and his goal would be ten thousand. And the following day the rock was the richest ever! As if to tantalize him into working on and on, the deeper he cut the richer the ore became. By nightfall of that day he had taken out more than a thousand dollars.

Now the lust of the gold was getting into him, taking him by the throat. He was fascinated by the danger of the tower as well as the desire for the gold. Three more days to go—could he leave it then? He looked again at the tower and felt a peculiar sense of foreboding, a feeling that here he was to die, that he would never escape. Was it his imagination, or had the outer wall leaned a little more?

On the morning of the twenty-second day he climbed the fan over a path that use had built into a series of continuous steps. He had never counted those steps but there must have been over a thousand of them. Dropping his canteen into a shaded hollow and pick in hand he started for the tower.

The forward tilt *did* seem somewhat more than before. Or was it the light? The crack that ran behind the outer wall seemed to have widened and when he examined it more closely he found a small pile of freshly run silt near the bottom of the crack. So it had moved!

Wetherton hesitated, staring at the rock with wary attention. He was a fool to go back in there again. Seven thousand dollars was more than he had ever had in his life before, yet in the next few hours he could take out at least a thousand dollars more and in the next three days he could easily have the ten thousand he had set for his goal.

He walked to the opening, dropped to his knees and crawled into the narrowing, flat-roofed hole. No sooner was he inside than fear climbed up into his throat. He felt trapped, stifled, but he fought down the mounting panic and began to work. His first blows were so frightened and feeble that nothing came loose. Yet, when he did get started, he began to work with a feverish intensity that was wholly unlike him.

When he slowed and then stopped to fill his sack he was gasping for breath, but despite his hurry the sack was not quite full. Reluctantly, he lifted his pick again, but before he could strike a blow, the gigantic mass above him seemed to creak like something tired and old. A deep shudder went through the

colossal pile and then a deep grinding that turned him sick
with horror. All his plans for instant flight were frozen and it
was not until the groaning ceased that he realized he was lying
on his back, breathless with fear and expectancy. Slowly, he
edged his way into the air and walked, fighting the desire to
run, away from the rock.

When he stopped near his canteen he was wringing with
cold sweat and trembling in every muscle. He sat down on the
rock and fought for control. It was not until some twenty
minutes had passed that he could trust himself to get to his
feet.

Despite his experience, he knew that if he did not go back
now he would never go. He had out but one sack for the day
and wanted another. Circling the batholith he examined the
widening crack, endeavoring again, for the third time, to find
another means of access to the vein.

The tilt of the outer wall was obvious, and it could stand no
more without toppling. It was possible that by cutting into the
wall of the column and striking down he might tap the vein at a
safer point. Yet this added blow at the foundation would bring
the tower nearer to collapse and render his other hole untenable.
Even this new attempt would not be safe, although immeasur-
ably more secure than the hole he had left. Hesitating, he
looked back at the hole.

Once more? The ore was now fabulously rich, and the few
pounds he needed to complete the sack he could get in just a
little while. He stared at the black and undoubtedly narrower
hole, then looked up at the leaning wall. He picked up his pick
and, his mouth dry, started back, drawn by a fascination that
was beyond all reason.

His heart pounding, he dropped to his knees at the tunnel
face. The air seemed stifling and he could feel his scalp tingling,
but once he started to crawl it was better. The face where he
now worked was at least sixteen feet from the tunnel mouth.
Pick in hand, he began to wedge chunks from their seat. The
going seemed harder now and the chunks did not come loose

so easily. Above him the tower made no sound. The crushing weight was now something tangible. He could almost feel it growing, increasing with every move of his. The mountain seemed resting on his shoulder, crushing the air from his lungs.

Suddenly he stopped. His sack almost full, he stopped and lay very still, staring up at the bulk of the rock above him.

No.

He would go no further. Now he would quit. Not another sackful. Not another pound. He would go out now. He would go down the mountain without a backward look, and he would keep going. His wife waiting at home, little Tommy, who would run gladly to meet him—these were too much to gamble.

With the decision came peace, came certainty. He sighed deeply, and relaxed, and then it seemed to him that every muscle in his body had been knotted with strain. He turned on his side and with great deliberation gathered his lantern, his sack, his hand-pick.

He had won. He had defeated the crumbling tower, he had defeated his own greed. He backed easily, without the caution that had marked his earlier movements in the cave. His blind, trusting foot found the projecting rock, a piece of quartz that stuck out from the rough-hewn wall.

The blow was too weak, too feeble to have brought forth the reaction that followed. The rock seemed to quiver like the flesh of a beast when stabbed; a queer vibration went through that ancient rock, then a deep, gasping sigh.

He had waited too long!

Fear came swiftly in upon him, crowding him, while his body twisted, contracting into the smallest possible space. He tried to will his muscles to move beneath the growing sounds that vibrated through the passage. The whispers of the rock grew into a terrifying groan, and there was a rattle of pebbles. Then silence.

The silence was more horrifying than the sound. Somehow

he was crawling, even as he expected the avalanche of gold to bury him. Abruptly, his feet were in the open. He was out.

He ran without stopping, but behind him he heard a growing roar that he couldn't outrace. When he knew from the slope of the land that he must be safe from falling rock, he fell to his knees. He turned and looked back. The muted, roaring sound, like thunder beyond mountains, continued, but there was no visible change in the tower. Suddenly, as he watched, the whole rock formation seemed to shift and tip. The movement lasted only seconds, but before the tons of rock had found their new equilibrium, his tunnel and the area around it had utterly vanished from sight.

When he could finally stand Wetherton gathered up his sack of ore and his canteen. The wind was cool upon his face as he walked away; and he did not look back again.

ONE FOR THE POT

When Laurie reached the water hole at Rustler's Springs she knew she had missed the trail.

Steve had explained about the shortcut across the mountains to Dry Creek Station, and had advised her to take it if anything happened to him. But he had warned her about riding near the Junipers or stopping at Rustler's Springs.

By retracing her trail she might discover the turnoff she had missed, but if she delayed any more it would be long after dark before she reached the stage station.

The logical move was to return to the ranch and make a fresh start at daybreak, as soon as Steve had left the house. Yet if she returned now she might never again muster the nerve to leave him. And she had already been too much trouble to Steve.

While the bay drank of the cool water Laurie slid from the saddle and tried dipping up a drink in the palm of her hand. The swallow of water was unsatisfactory and all she succeeded in doing was getting her face wet and spilling water on her blouse. It was somehow symbolic of all her failures since coming west.

When she got to her feet there was a man standing at the edge of the brush with a rifle cradled in his arms. How long he had been there she had no idea, but suddenly she was keenly aware of the utter loneliness of the spot and that not even Steve knew where she was. And her only weapon was the pistol in her saddlebag.

The man was thin and old with white hair and the coldest eyes she had ever seen looking from a human face. Tiny wrinkles wove a pattern of harsh years across the sun-darkened patina of his skin. It was a narrow face, high in the cheekbones . . . a hawk's face except for the blunted nose. His blue shirt was faded, his jeans worn. Only the narrow-brimmed hat was new.

He did not speak, merely stared at her and waited.

"I missed the shortcut," she was surprised that she could speak so calmly. "I was going to Dry Creek Station."

His eyes left her face for the carpetbag behind her saddle. It contained only the few belongings she had brought to Red Tanks Ranch and to Steve Bonnet.

"You're Bonnet's woman," he said then. His voice was thin and dry.

Her chin lifted. "His wife."

"Quittin' him?"

Resentment flared. "It's none of your business!"

"Don't blame you for bein' skeered."

"It's not that!" she protested. "It's not that at all!"

His eyes had grown old in the reading of trail sign and the motives of men—and women.

She did not lie. Something other than fear was driving her. He could sense the bitterness in her, the sense of failure, and the hurt.

His head jerked toward the south. "Cabin's over there," he said, "and coffee's on."

Afterward she was to wonder why she followed him. Perhaps it was to show him she was not afraid, or it might have been hesitation to cross that last bridge that would take her from this country and the promise it had held for her.

The cabin was old but neat. There were bunks for several men, empty of bedding save one. The bed was neatly made and the few utensils were clean and hung in place.

Filling two enamel cups he placed one before her. Tasting the coffee she felt envy for the first time. For this had been her greatest failure. At least, it was the failure she was most miserable about. She could not make good coffee, not even good enough to please herself.

It had not taken her long to discover that she was not cut out to be the wife of a western man, but it was a mistake she could now rectify.

With a little pang she remembered Steve's face when he saw the sore on the gelding's back. A wrinkle carelessly left in her saddle blanket had done that. Then there was the time his spare pistol had gone off in her hand, narrowly missing her foot. He had been furious with her, and she had cried most of the night after he was asleep.

"Surprised you'd take out on your man," the old man said, "didn't figure you for skeered after you throwed down on Big Lew with that shotgun."

She looked up, surprised at his knowledge. "But why should he frighten me? Besides," she added, "the shotgun wasn't loaded."

The cold eyes glinted with what might have been humor. "That'll jolt Lew. You had him right buffalocd."

He pushed the coffeepot back on the fire. "Took nerve. Lew ain't no pilgrim. He's killed hisself a few men."

"He really has?"

"Three, maybe four." He stoked his pipe, glancing out of the corners of his eyes at her face. It was a small, heart-shaped face with large, dark eyes, and her body, while a beautifully shaped woman's body, seemed almost too small, too childlike for this country. Yet his mother had been a small woman, and she had borne ten children in a rugged, frontier community. "If you ain't skeered, why you takin' out?" Then his eyes crinkled at the corners and he said wryly, "But I forgit. That ain't none of my business."

"I'm no good to him," she looked up, her dark eyes wide. "He needs someone who can help. All I do is make trouble for him."

The old man looked thoughtfully at his pipe. Her presence with that shotgun had prevented Big Lew and the Millers from burning the ranch. That had been their purpose in going to Red Tanks.

Little by little her story came out. Her father's long illness had absorbed their savings, and after his death she had become a mail-order wife. Steve Bonnet had needed a wife, and when she got off the stage and saw the tall, silent young man with the sun-bronzed face she had felt a queer little quiver of excitement. He needed a wife, she needed a home. It had been simple as that. They had not talked of love.

"In love with him now?"

The question startled her for she had not given it a thought. Suddenly she realized, shocking as it was . . . "Yes," she acknowledged. "I am."

The old man said nothing then, and she watched the shadows of the trees on the ground outside the cabin. She remembered Steve's face when he had come home the night before, the something in his eyes when he saw her. Had it been relief? Pleasure? What?

He refilled her cup. "Will quittin' give you rest? And how will he feel when he comes home tonight?"

She stifled the pang. "He's better off without me."

"Nothin' nice about comin' home to an empty house. You told him you love him?"

"No."

"He told you?"

"No."

"Wrong of him. Knowed a sight of women, here 'n there. Tell 'em you love 'em, pet 'em a mite, do somethin' unexpected nice time to time an' they'll break their necks for you."

The cottonwoods brushed their pale green palms together, rustling in the still, hot afternoon. "I wish I could make coffee like this."

"Not's good as usual." She noticed how the rifle lay where he had placed it, across the corner of the table, pointing a finger at the door. "Helps to have hot coffee when a man gets to home."

He leaned back in his chair and lighted his pipe again. "He know you're gone?"

"No."

"If them Millers come back they could burn him out. And him countin' on you."

"They won't come back."

His reply was a snort of contempt for such ignorance. "This here's a war, ma'am. It's a fight for range . . . and you're the only one your man's got on his side . . . and you quittin'."

"I'm no good to him. I can't do any of the things a wife should do out here."

"You can be home when he gets there. No man likes to stand alone. It's a sight of comfort for a man to know he's fightin' *for* something."

When she remained silent he said quietly, "They figure to have him killed, them Millers do."

"Killed?" She was shocked. "Why, the law . . ."

He looked at her, cold-eyed. "A man carries his law in his holster in this country. Them Millers don't want no part of Steve Bonnet themselves. They hire their killin' done when it's somebody like him. That man of yours," the old man got to his feet, "is plumb salty."

He was suddenly impatient. "You ain't only a wife. You're a pardner, and you're quittin' when he needs you most."

He started for the door. "No need to go back to Six-shooter Gap. There's a trail back of here that old Stockton used. You stay shut of the Junipers and hold to the trail. It'll take you right to the stage station. You'll hit it near Little Dry."

She did not move. "Will you teach me how to make coffee like that?"

*   *   *

A quail was calling when she rode into the yard at Red Tanks. Steve was not back, and she hurriedly stripped the saddle from the gelding. Then, remembering what Steve had done, she rubbed the horse down.

An hour later, her second batch of coffee hot and ready, she watched Steve ride into the yard. When she thought how she had nearly failed to be here to greet him she felt a queer little wrench of dismay, and she stood there in the door, seeing him suddenly with new eyes.

This was the man she loved. This man, this tall, narrow-hipped man with the quiet face and the faintly amused eyes. His bronzed hair glinted in the light as he stepped into the door, but there was no amusement in his eyes now. They were shadowed with worry.

"Steve . . . what's wrong?"

He looked at her suddenly, as if detecting a new ring in her voice. And for the first time he shared his troubles with her. Before he had always brushed off her questions, assuring her everything would be all right.

"Heard somethin' today. Old Man Miller has hired a man. A killer."

She caught his arm. "Steve? For you?"

He nodded, closing the door. He took off his hat and started for the wash basin. Then he smelled the coffee and saw the cup freshly poured.

He looked up at her. "Mine?"

She nodded, almost afraid for him to try it. Such a little thing, yet a mark for or against her.

He dropped into the chair and she saw the sudden weariness in his face. He tasted the coffee, then drank.

"A man named Bud Shaw. He's already here."

"You've seen him?"

"Not around here." He was drinking his coffee. "I saw him in El Paso once, when I first came west. He's a known man."

"But he kills for money? They can really hire men to kill someone?"

"This is a hard country, Laurie, and there's a war for range.

Men hire out to fight as they join armies of other countries. I don't know as I blame 'em much."

Laurie was indignant. "But to kill for money! Why, that's murder!"

Steve looked up quickly. "Yes, if they drygulch a man. Bud Shaw won't do that. He'll meet me somewhere, unexpected like, and I'll have my chance." He got up. "I shouldn't be telling you this. The country's rough on womenfolks."

He glanced at his empty cup. "Say, how about some more coffee?"

For a long time she lay awake. How like a little boy he looked! In the vague light from the moon she could see his face against the pillow, his hair tousled, his breathing even and steady. Suddenly, on impulse, she touched his cheek. Almost frightened, she drew her hand back quickly, then slid deeper under the coarse blankets and lay there, her eyes wide open, her heart beating fast.

When breakfast was over and he had picked up his rifle, she stopped him suddenly. "Steve . . . teach me to load the shotgun."

He looked around at her and for an instant their eyes held. Suddenly, his cheeks flushed. He turned back and picked up the shotgun, but his eyes avoided hers. Carefully, he showed her how the shotgun functioned, then at the door, he pointed. "See that white rock? If they come here, stop 'em beyond that. If they come closer . . . shoot."

She nodded seriously, and he looked at her again, and suddenly he gripped her shoulder hard. "You'll do, Laurie," he said quietly, his voice shaken, "you'll do."

She was sitting where she could see out the door and down the trail when she heard the horse. She got up quickly and put her sewing aside. Heart pounding, she went to the door.

It was a lone man, riding a mouse-gray horse. A shabby old man, but he wore a neat, narrow-brimmed hat.

He stopped on the edge of the woods and sat his horse there, one hand on the rifle, watching the door. He let his eyes drift slowly over the place, but she had a curious feeling that he was watching her, too, all the time his gaze wandered.

Then he let the horse walk forward and when he stopped he looked at her. "Howdy, ma'am. Mind if I git down?"

"Please do." He swung down, then leaving his horse ground hitched, he walked up to the door. "Passin' by," he said, "and I reckoned I'd try some of that there coffee."

When he was seated she poured a cup, and watched his expression anxiously. He tried it, tasted it again, then nodded. "A mite more coffee, ma'am, and you got it."

He looked around the neat little cabin, then out over the yard. The corrals were new and well built, the cabin was solidly constructed and the stable was no makeshift.

"Seen anything of Big Lew Miller?"

"No." She looked at him suddenly. "Look, did you ever hear of a man named Bud Shaw? He's a killer. A man with a gun for hire."

The old man touched his mustache thoughtfully. "Bud Shaw? The name seems sort of familiar." He looked up at her, his eyes veiled and cold. "A killer, you say? Where did you hear that?"

"Steve told me today. Oh, he said that this man Bud Shaw was different than some, that he'd give a man a chance before he killed him. But I don't think that matters.

"Look," she leaned toward him, "you know outlaws. If you didn't, you wouldn't be living at Rustler's Springs. At least, Steve says that's a hangout for them. If you know how I can meet Bud Shaw and talk to him, I wish you'd fix it up."

He drank coffee and then rolled a smoke. She watched the slim brown fingers, almost like a woman's. Not one shred of tobacco spilled on the floor. When he had touched his tongue to the cigarette he looked around at her. "What you want to see him for?"

She had a notion of talking to him. No man could be so cruel as to—well, it wasn't right to shoot people, and Steve was a good man, only trying to build a home. That's all. And he wanted children, and . . . she was explaining all this when he interrupted.

"I take it you've changed your mind about runnin' off?"

She flushed. "I—I must have been mad. He does need me. You believe that, don't you? I mean—you think he really does?"

At the last her voice was pleading.

"A man needs a woman. No man is right without one, believe me. And with Steve it's got to be the right woman. He's that kind of man."

"But you said you didn't know him?"

"I don't. Not rightly, I don't. But folks hear things." His voice was suddenly sour. "Lady, Steve Bonnet won't kill easy. Not for Bud Shaw or nobody. Why do you reckon the Millers ain't killed him? There's four Millers. Why ain't they done it?"

He struck a match and lighted his smoke. "The Millers tried it, but there was five of them, then. Your husband killed one Miller and put another in the hospital."

Steve had killed a man. Somehow the fact was not so shocking as it might have been a day or two before. Probably that was why he hesitated to condemn even a hired killer.

The old man got to his feet. "I'm driftin', ma'am. See you sometime."

"Wait." She went to the cupboard and hurriedly took down a pan of biscuits. "I just baked these, and some bread. Take them along." She took a brown loaf from the cupboard and put it with the biscuits into a sack. "That is one thing I can do!" Her chin lifted a little. "I can bake bread."

The old man looked at her thoughtfully. "Thanks, ma'am. I appreciate this. First time anybody has given me anything for a long time."

"And don't forget, you promised to come over and teach me how to make soap."

He actually smiled. "Sure enough, I did at that."

When he was gone she looked down the trail again. And returning to her chair, resumed her work.

It was almost dusk when she saw the rider. For an instant she was sure it was Steve, and then he vanished into the trees.

Quickly, she got up, closed the window shutters and got the shotgun. Then she put out the light and waited. It was not yet dark outside and she could see clearly.

A long time later a soft rustle outside the window caused her shotgun to lift. A man rounded into the door and her finger was tightening on her trigger when she recognized Steve.

Frightened, she got to her feet. "Oh, Steve! I might have shot you!"

He glanced at her, his eyes wary. "You're alone?"

"Why—of course! Who would be here?"

He walked to the bedroom and drew back the blanket that curtained the door. When he returned to the kitchen he paused, looking around. "Somebody scouted the place today. A man ridin' a small horse."

She started to explain, then caught herself. If she told about the friendly old man then she must explain how they had met, and that she had planned to leave Steve. That she could not bring herself to do. Not now.

He was watching her, an odd look in his eyes. Her hesitation had aroused his doubts.

"It must have been a mistake," she said guiltily. "I saw no one."

Her voice trailed off, but she knew she was a poor liar. Steve dropped into a chair and looked at her, frowning a little. To avoid his eyes she hastily began to put food on the table, and then, desperately, tried to open a conversation. Somehow her words trailed off into nothing.

Each time their eyes met, Steve deliberately looked away.

"Steve—what's wrong?"

He did not meet her eyes. He got up. "Nothin'. Just tired, I guess."

At daylight she was up and she got breakfast, her heart tight and cold within her. Steve said nothing, only once when he finished combing his hair and turned away from the glass, their eyes met. His face looked drawn and lonely. Laurie longed to run to him and . . .

"You be careful," he said, sitting down at the table. "Don't let anybody in here. The Millers—they might try anything."

"Have you seen that other man?"

"Shaw?" He shook his head, watching her fill his cup. "No. He's the one worries me. That was no Miller horse that I tracked. That Shaw—he might try anything. All a man knows is that he'll be where he's least expected."

He waited inside the door for a long time before he went to the stable. He stood there, just studying the place, the trees, the hills. Reluctantly, he stepped out and then moved to the stable, flattened against the wall, then went in.

She waited breathless for him to emerge. When he came out he took a quick look toward the house.

He did not trust her. Laurie knew that now. He believed . . . but what could he believe?

Suddenly, she started out. "Steve!" She ran toward him. "Steve! Don't go!"

He hesitated. "Work to be done. If I hide today, what about tomorrow, and the next day? I can't hide all the time. I got to go on."

The old man came up to the house just before sundown and he was walking, carrying his inevitable rifle. He came up to the door and waited until she saw him.

"Ma'am, I got to talk to you."

"You'd better go away." Laurie's small face was stiff with worry. "Steve saw your tracks. He—doesn't trust me."

"You told him about me? You described me?" he asked quickly.

"No. I told him I had seen no one. He didn't believe me."

"I got to come inside, ma'am. Right away. I got to get out of sight."

She looked at him, saw the queer tightness in the parchment-like brown skin. She hesitated only a moment, then stepped aside. "You'll help us?"

"I'll help you."

"Against Bud Shaw, too?"

He looked at her. "Yes," he said wryly, "even against him."

Then they heard the horse. A lone horse, and he was coming

fast. From somewhere a shot sounded, then a volley. Then another shot.

The old man swore viciously. He started forward, then shrank back.

It was the gelding, and Steve Bonnet was clinging to the saddle horn. He half-fell from the saddle and, with a start of horror, Laurie saw the blood on his shirt and face, blood on his sleeve. He lunged, tripped on the step, and then before she could move to help him, he scrambled into the door. "Laurie!" His voice was hoarse. "The shotgun! They're comin'!"

He grasped the door edge and half-turned, and then he saw the man standing by the table.

Laurie saw a sudden stillness come over his face, a strange coolness. His one good hand, his left, halted above the gun in his waistband. The butt was turned for a right hand draw . . . it was an awkward chance.

"Hello, Bud," he said quietly.

Laurie cried out, a stabbing little cry.

"Hello, Steve."

The man waited, looking at Steve.

"Go ahead," Steve said bitterly. "You've given me my chance. I'm ready."

Bud Shaw looked at him, and nodded gravely. "Sure you are, Steve. I knew that. You'd always be ready." He waited and Laurie could hear the clock tick, and somewhere outside the slow movement of approaching horses with cautious riders.

"You're a lucky man, Steve," Bud said quietly, "you've got a game wife, a fine wife."

Slowly then, with conscious and obvious deliberation he turned and went out the door. He stopped there with his feet wide.

They heard the horses coming on, then heard them stop. Steve stared at Laurie, listening. Then he dropped his hand for the shotgun and lifted it. She could see the blood on his sleeve, reddening his right hand.

"All right, Lew," it was Bud Shaw speaking, "you can stop right there."

"Never knowed you for a turncoat, Bud," Big Lew spoke carefully.

"I told you I was through," Bud Shaw spoke reasonably, "I told you plain."

"You said nothin' about switchin' sides."

"Well, then. Hear it now. I've switched. If you want to know why, I'll tell you. Two things made me switch. Four yellow bellies that had to hire their killin', and then drygulched a lone man. That was only part of it."

They could see him standing there, a slight old man, his shoulders thin under the worn shirt. He had left the rifle inside and stood there with the two sixguns on his belt, facing them.

"The other thing was a little lady who wanted nothin' so much as to make good coffee for her man. I figure the man that little lady could love was too much of a man to be shot down for a pack of coyotes."

Big Lew's voice was harsh. "We won't take that talk, Bud! Not even from you!"

"You'll take it," the old man's voice was dry with patience and disgust, "you'll take it, and I more than half wish you wouldn't."

He stood there like that in the gathering dusk and watched them ride away. When Laurie moved close to Steve and put her arm around him, she did not know, but she was there when the old man turned back to the door.

"Light the light, Laurie," he said gently, "and let's have a look at that shoulder."

WAR PARTY

We buried pa on a sidehill out west of camp, buried him high up so his ghost could look down the trail he'd planned to travel.

We piled the grave high with rocks because of the coyotes, and we dug the grave deep, and some of it I dug myself, and Mr. Sampson helped, and some others.

Folks in the wagon train figured ma would turn back, but they hadn't known ma so long as I had. Once she set her mind to something she wasn't about to quit.

She was a young woman and pretty, but there was strength in her. She was a lone woman with two children, but she was of no mind to turn back. She'd come through the Little Crow massacre in Minnesota and she knew what trouble was. Yet it was like her that she put it up to me.

"Bud," she said, when we were alone, "we can turn back, but we've nobody there who cares about us, and it's of you and Jeanie that I'm thinking. If we go west you will have to be the man of the house, and you'll have to work hard to make up for pa."

24

"We'll go west," I said. A boy those days took it for granted that he had work to do, and the men couldn't do it all. No boy ever thought of himself as only twelve or thirteen or whatever he was, being anxious to prove himself a man, and take a man's place and responsibilities.

Ryerson and his wife were going back. She was a complaining woman and he was a man who was always ailing when there was work to be done. Four or five wagons were turning back, folks with their tails betwixt their legs running for the shelter of towns where their own littleness wouldn't stand out so plain.

When a body crossed the Mississippi and left the settlements behind, something happened to him. The world seemed to bust wide open, and suddenly the horizons spread out and a man wasn't cramped anymore. The pinched-up villages and the narrowness of towns, all that was gone. The horizons simply exploded and rolled back into enormous distance, with nothing around but prairie and sky.

Some folks couldn't stand it. They'd cringe into themselves and start hunting excuses to go back where they came from. This was a big country needing big men and women to live in it, and there was no place out here for the frightened or the mean.

The prairie and sky had a way of trimming folks down to size, or changing them to giants to whom nothing seemed impossible. Men who had cut a wide swath back in the States found themselves nothing out here. They were folks who were used to doing a lot of talking who suddenly found that no one was listening anymore, and things that seemed mighty important back home, like family and money, they amounted to nothing alongside character and courage.

There was John Sampson from our town. He was a man used to being told to do things, used to looking up to wealth and power, but when he crossed the Mississippi he began to lift his head and look around. He squared his shoulders, put more crack to his whip and began to make his own tracks in the land.

Pa was always strong, an independent man given to reading at night from one of the four or five books we had, to speaking up on matters of principle and to straight shooting with a rifle. Pa had fought the Comanche and lived with the Sioux, but he wasn't strong enough to last more than two days with a Kiowa arrow through his lung. But he died knowing ma had stood by the rear wheel and shot the Kiowa whose arrow it was.

Right then I knew that neither Indians nor country was going to get the better of ma. Shooting that Kiowa was the first time ma had shot anything but some chicken-killing varmint— which she'd done time to time when pa was away from home.

Only ma wouldn't let Jeanie and me call it home. "We came here from Illinois," she said, "but we're going home now."

"But, ma," I protested, "I thought home was where we came from?"

"Home is where we're going now," ma said, "and we'll know it when we find it. Now that pa is gone we'll have to build that home ourselves."

She had a way of saying "home" so it sounded like a rare and wonderful place and kept Jeanie and me looking always at the horizon, just knowing it was over there, waiting for us to see it. She had given us the dream, and even Jeanie, who was only six, she had it too.

She might tell us that home was where we were going, but I knew home was where ma was, a warm and friendly place with biscuits on the table and fresh-made butter. We wouldn't have a real home until ma was there and we had a fire going. Only I'd build the fire.

Mr. Buchanan, who was captain of the wagon train, came to us with Tryon Burt, who was guide. "We'll help you," Mr. Buchanan said. "I know you'll be wanting to go back, and——"

"But we are not going back." Ma smiled at them. "And don't be afraid we'll be a burden. I know you have troubles of your own, and we will manage very well."

Mr. Buchanan looked uncomfortable, like he was trying to think of the right thing to say. "Now, see here," he protested, "we started this trip with a rule. There has to be a man with every wagon."

Ma put her hand on my shoulder. "I have my man. Bud is

almost thirteen and accepts responsibility. I could ask for no better man."

Ryerson came up. He was thin, stooped in the shoulder, and whenever he looked at ma there was a greasy look to his eyes that I didn't like. He was a man who looked dirty even when he'd just washed in the creek. "You come along with me, ma'am," he said. "I'll take good care of you."

"Mr. Ryerson"—ma looked him right in the eye—"you have a wife who can use better care than she's getting, and I have my son."

"He's nothin' but a boy."

"You are turning back, are you not? My son is going on. I believe that should indicate who is more the man. It is neither size nor age that makes a man, Mr. Ryerson, but something he has inside. My son has it."

Ryerson might have said something unpleasant only Tryon Burt was standing there wishing he would, so he just looked ugly and hustled off.

"I'd like to say you could come," Mr. Buchanan said, "but the boy couldn't stand up to a man's work."

Ma smiled at him, chin up, the way she had. "I do not believe in gambling, Mr. Buchanan, but I'll wager a good Ballard rifle there isn't a man in camp who could follow a child all day, running when it runs, squatting when it squats, bending when it bends and wrestling when it wrestles and not be played out long before the child is."

"You may be right, ma'am, but a rule is a rule."

"We are in Indian country, Mr. Buchanan. If you are killed a week from now, I suppose your wife must return to the States?"

"That's different! Nobody could turn back from there!"

"Then," ma said sweetly, "it seems a rule is only a rule within certain limits, and if I recall correctly no such limit was designated in the articles of travel. Whatever limits there were, Mr. Buchanan, must have passed sometime before the Indian attack that killed my husband."

"I can drive the wagon, and so can ma," I said. "For the past two days I've been driving, and nobody said anything until pa died."

Mr. Buchanan didn't know what to say, but a body could see he didn't like it. Nor did he like a woman who talked up to him the way ma did.

Tryon Burt spoke up. "Let the boy drive. I've watched this youngster, and he'll do. He has better judgment than most men in the outfit, and he stands up to his work. If need be, I'll help."

Mr. Buchanan turned around and walked off with his back stiff the way it is when he's mad. Ma looked at Burt, and she said, "Thank you, Mr. Burt. That was nice of you."

Try Burt, he got all red around the gills and took off like somebody had put a burr under his saddle.

Come morning our wagon was the second one ready to take its place in line, with both horses saddled and tied behind the wagon, and me standing beside the off ox.

Any direction a man wanted to look there was nothing but grass and sky, only sometimes there'd be a buffalo wallow or a gopher hole. We made eleven miles the first day after pa was buried, sixteen the next, then nineteen, thirteen and twenty-one. At no time did the country change. On the sixth day after pa died I killed a buffalo.

It was a young bull, but a big one, and I spotted him coming up out of a draw and was off my horse and bellied down in the grass before Try Burt realized there was game in sight. That bull came up from the draw and stopped there, staring at the wagon train, which was a half-mile off. Setting a sight behind his left shoulder I took a long breath, took in the trigger slack, then squeezed off my shot so gentle-like the gun jumped in my hands before I was ready for it.

The bull took a step back like something had surprised him, and I jacked another shell into the chamber and was sighting on him again when he went down on his knees and rolled over on his side.

"You got him, Bud!" Burt was more excited than me. "That was shootin'!"

Try got down and showed me how to skin the bull, and lent me a hand. Then we cut out a lot of fresh meat and toted it back to the wagons.

Ma was at the fire when we came up, a wisp of brown hair alongside her cheek and her face flushed from the heat of the fire, looking as pretty as a bay pony.

"Bud killed his first buffalo," Burt told her, looking at ma like he could eat her with a spoon.

"Why, Bud! That's wonderful!" Her eyes started to dance with a kind of mischief in them, and she said, "Bud, why don't you take a piece of that meat along to Mr. Buchanan and the others?"

With Burt to help, we cut the meat into eighteen pieces and distributed it around the wagons. It wasn't much, but it was the first fresh meat in a couple of weeks.

John Sampson squeezed my shoulder and said, "Seems to me you and your ma are folks to travel with. This outfit needs some hunters."

Each night I staked out that buffalo hide, and each day I worked at curing it before rolling it up to pack on the wagon. Believe you me, I was some proud of that buffalo hide. Biggest thing I'd shot until then was a cottontail rabbit back in Illinois, where we lived when I was born. Try Burt told folks about that shot. "Two hundred yards," he'd say, "right through the heart."

Only it wasn't more than a hundred and fifty yards the way I figured, and pa used to make me pace off distances, so I'd learn to judge right. But I was nobody to argue with Try Burt telling a story—besides, two hundred yards makes an awful lot better sound than one hundred and fifty.

After supper the menfolks would gather to talk plans. The season was late, and we weren't making the time we ought if we hoped to beat the snow through the passes of the Sierras. When they talked I was there because I was the man of my wagon, but nobody paid me no mind. Mr. Buchanan, he acted like he didn't see me, but John Sampson would not, and Try Burt always smiled at me.

Several spoke up for turning back, but Mr. Buchanan said he knew of an outfit that made it through later than this. One thing was sure. Our wagon wasn't turning back. Like ma said, home was somewhere ahead of us, and back in the States we'd have no money and nobody to turn to, nor any relatives, anywhere. It was the three of us.

"We're going on," I said at one of these talks. "We don't figure to turn back for anything."

Webb gave me a glance full of contempt. "You'll go where the rest of us go. You an' your ma would play hob gettin' by on your own."

Next day it rained, dawn to dark it fairly poured, and we were lucky to make six miles. Day after that, with the wagon wheels sinking into the prairie and the rain still falling, we camped just two miles from where we started in the morning.

Nobody talked much around the fires, and what was said was apt to be short and irritable. Most of these folks had put all they owned into the outfits they had, and if they turned back now they'd have nothing to live on and nothing left to make a fresh start. Except a few like Mr. Buchanan, who was well off.

"It doesn't have to be California," ma said once. "What most of us want is land, not gold."

"This here is Indian country," John Sampson said, "and a sight too open for me. I'd like a valley in the hills, with running water close by."

"There will be valleys and meadows," ma replied, stirring the stew she was making, "and tall trees near running streams, and tall grass growing in the meadows, and there will be game in the forest and on the grassy plains, and places for homes."

"And where will we find all that?" Webb's tone was slighting.

"West," ma said, "over against the mountains."

"I suppose you've been there?" Webb scoffed.

"No, Mr. Webb, I haven't been there, but I've been told of it. The land is there, and we will have some of it, my children and I, and we will stay through the winter, and in the spring we will plant our crops."

"Easy to say."

"This is Sioux country to the north," Burt said. "We'll be lucky to get through without a fight. There was a war party of thirty or thirty-five passed this way a couple of days ago."

"Sioux?"

"Uh-huh—no women or children along, and I found where some war paint rubbed off on the brush."

"Maybe," Mr. Buchanan suggested, "we'd better turn south a mite."

"It is late in the season," ma replied, "and the straightest way is the best way now."

"No use to worry," White interrupted; "those Indians went on by. They won't likely know we're around."

"They were riding southeast," ma said, "and their home is in the north, so when they return they'll be riding northwest. There is no way they can miss our trail."

"Then we'd best turn back," White said.

"Don't look like we'd make it this year, anyway," a woman said; "the season is late."

That started the argument, and some were for turning back and some wanted to push on, and finally White said they should push on, but travel fast.

"Fast?" Webb asked disparagingly. "An Indian can ride in one day the distance we'd travel in four."

That started the wrangling again and ma continued with her cooking. Sitting there watching her I figured I never did see anybody so graceful or quick on her feet as ma, and when we used to walk in the woods back home I never knew her to stumble or step on a fallen twig or branch.

The group broke up and returned to their own fires with nothing settled, only there at the end Mr. Buchanan looked to Burt. "Do you know the Sioux?"

"Only the Utes and Shoshonis, and I spent a winter on the Snake with the Nez Percés one time. But I've had no truck with the Sioux. Only they tell me they're bad medicine. Fightin' men from way back and they don't cotton to white folks in their country. If we run into Sioux, we're in trouble."

After Mr. Buchanan had gone Tryon Burt accepted a plate and cup from ma and settled down to eating. After a while he looked up at her and said, "Beggin' your pardon, ma'am, but it struck me you knew a sight about trackin' for an Eastern woman. You'd spotted those Sioux your own self, an' you figured it right that they'd pick up our trail on the way back."

She smiled at him. "It was simply an observation, Mr. Burt. I would believe anyone would notice it. I simply put it into words."

Burt went on eating, but he was mighty thoughtful, and it didn't seem to me he was satisfied with ma's answer. Ma said finally, "It seems to be raining west of here. Isn't it likely to be snowing in the mountains?"

Burt looked up uneasily. "Not necessarily so, ma'am. It could be raining here and not snowing there, but I'd say there was a chance of snow." He got up and came around the fire to the coffeepot. "What are you gettin' at, ma'am?"

"Some of them are ready to turn back or change their plans. What will you do then?"

He frowned, placing his cup on the grass and starting to fill his pipe. "No idea—might head south for Santa Fe. Why do you ask?"

"Because we're going on," ma said. "We're going to the mountains, and I am hoping some of the others decide to come with us."

"You'd go alone?" He was amazed.

"If necessary."

We started on at daybreak, but folks were more scary than before, and they kept looking at the great distances stretching away on either side, and muttering. There was an autumn coolness in the air, and we were still short of South Pass by several days with the memory of the Donner party being talked up around us.

There was another kind of talk in the wagons, and some of it I heard. The nightly gatherings around ma's fire had started talk, and some of it pointed to Tryon Burt, and some were saying other things.

We made seventeen miles that day, and at night Mr. Buchanan didn't come to our fire; and when White stopped by, his wife came and got him. Ma looked at her and smiled, and Mrs. White sniffed and went away beside her husband.

"Mr. Burt"—ma wasn't one to beat around a bush—"is there talk about me?"

Try Burt got red around the ears and he opened his mouth, but couldn't find the words he wanted. "Maybe—well, maybe I shouldn't eat here all the time. Only—well, ma'am, you're the best cook in camp."

Ma smiled at him. "I hope that isn't the only reason you come to see us, Mr. Burt."

He got redder than ever then and gulped his coffee and took off in a hurry.

Time to time the men had stopped by to help a little, but next morning nobody came by. We got lined out about as soon as ever, and ma said to me as we sat on the wagon seat, "Pay no attention, Bud. You've no call to take up anything if you don't notice it. There will always be folks who will talk, and the better you do in the world the more bad things they will say of you. Back there in the settlement you remember how the dogs used to run out and bark at our wagons?"

"Yes, ma."

"Did the wagons stop?"

"No, ma."

"Remember that, son. The dogs bark, but the wagons go on their way, and if you're going someplace you haven't time to bother with barking dogs."

We made eighteen miles that day, and the grass was better, but there was a rumble of distant thunder, whimpering and muttering off in the canyons, promising rain.

Webb stopped by, dropped an armful of wood beside the fire, then started off.

"Thank you, Mr. Webb," ma said, "but aren't you afraid you'll be talked about?"

He looked angry and started to reply something angry, and then he grinned and said, "I reckon I'd be flattered, Mrs. Miles."

Ma said, "No matter what is decided by the rest of them, Mr. Webb, we are going on, but there is no need to go to California for what we want."

Webb took out his pipe and tamped it. He had a dark, devil's face on him with eyebrows like you see on pictures of the devil. I was afraid of Mr. Webb.

"We want land," ma said, "and there is land around us. In the mountains ahead there will be streams and forests, there will be fish and game, logs for houses and meadows for grazing."

Mr. Buchanan had joined us. "That's fool talk," he declared. "What could anyone do in these hills? You'd be cut off from the world. Left out of it."

"A man wouldn't be so crowded as in California," John Sampson remarked. "I've seen so many go that I've been wondering what they all do there."

"For a woman," Webb replied, ignoring the others, "you've a head on you, ma'am."

"What about the Sioux?" Mr. Buchanan asked dryly.

"We'd not be encroaching on their land. They live to the north," ma said. She gestured toward the mountains. "There is land to be had just a few days further on, and that is where our wagon will stop."

A few days! Everybody looked at everybody else. Not months, but days only. Those who stopped then would have enough of their supplies left to help them through the winter, and with what game they could kill—and time for cutting wood and even building cabins before the cold set in.

Oh, there was an argument, such argument as you've never heard, and the upshot of it was that all agreed it was fool talk and the thing to do was keep going. And there was talk I overheard about ma being no better than she should be, and why was that guide always hanging around her? And all those men? No decent woman—I hurried away.

At break of day our wagons rolled down a long valley with a small stream alongside the trail, and the Indians came over the ridge to the south of us and started our way—tall, fine-looking men with feathers in their hair.

There was barely time for a circle, but I was riding off in front with Tryon Burt, and he said, "A man can always try to talk first, and Injuns like palaver. You get back to the wagons."

Only I rode along beside him, my rifle over my saddle and ready to hand. My mouth was dry and my heart was beating so's I thought Try could hear it, I was that scared. But behind us the wagons were making their circle, and every second was important.

Their chief was a big man with splendid muscles, and there was a scalp not many days old hanging from his lance. It looked like Ryerson's hair, but Ryerson's wagons should have been miles away to the east by now.

Burt tried them in Shoshoni, but it was the language of their enemies and they merely stared at him, understanding well enough, but of no mind to talk. One young buck kept staring at Burt with a taunt in his eye, daring Burt to make a move; then suddenly the chief spoke, and they all turned their eyes toward the wagons.

There was a rider coming, and it was a woman. It was ma.

She rode right up beside us, and when she drew up she started to talk, and she was speaking their language. She was talking Sioux. We both knew what it was because those Indians sat up and paid attention. Suddenly she directed a question at the chief.

"Red Horse," he said, in English.

Ma shifted to English. "My husband was blood brother to Gall, the greatest warrior of the Sioux nation. It was my husband who found Gall dying in the brush with a bayonet wound in his chest, who took Gall to his home and treated the wound until it was well."

"Your husband was a medicine man?" Red Horse asked.

"My husband was a warrior," ma replied proudly, "but he made war only against strong men, not women or children or the wounded."

She put her hand on my shoulder. "This is my son. As my husband was blood brother to Gall, his son is by blood brotherhood the son of Gall, also."

Red Horse stared at ma for a long time, and I was getting even more scared. I could feel a drop of sweat start at my collar and crawl slowly down my spine. Red Horse looked at me. "Is this one a fit son for Gall?"

"He is a fit son. He has killed his first buffalo."

Red Horse turned his mount and spoke to the others. One of

the young braves shouted angrily at him, and Red Horse replied sharply. Reluctantly, the warrior trailed off after their chief.

"Ma'am," Burt said, "you just about saved our bacon. They were just spoilin' for a fight."

"We should be moving," ma said.

Mr. Buchanan was waiting for us. "What happened out there? I tried to keep her back, but she's a difficult woman."

"She's worth any three men in the outfit," Burt replied.

That day we made eighteen miles, and by the time the wagons circled there was talk. The fact that ma had saved them was less important now than other things. It didn't seem right that a decent woman could talk Sioux or mix in the affairs of men.

Nobody came to our fire, but while picking the saddle horses I heard someone say, "Must be part Injun. Else why would they pay attention to a woman?"

"Maybe she's part Injun and leadin' us into a trap."

"Hadn't been for her," Burt said, "you'd all be dead now."

"How do you know what she said to 'em? Who savvies that lingo?"

"I never did trust that woman," Mrs. White said; "too high and mighty. Nor that husband of hers, either, comes to that. Kept to himself too much."

The air was cool after a brief shower when we started in the morning, and no Indians in sight. All day long we moved over grass made fresh by new rain, and all the ridges were pine-clad now, and the growth along the streams heavier. Short of sun-down I killed an antelope with a running shot, dropped him mighty neat—and looked up to see an Indian watching from a hill. At the distance I couldn't tell, but it could have been Red Horse.

Time to time I'd passed along the train, but nobody waved or said anything. Webb watched me go by, his face stolid as one of the Sioux, yet I could see there was a deal of talk going on.

"Why are they mad at us?" I asked Burt.

"Folks hate something they don't understand, or anything

seems different. Your ma goes her own way, speaks her mind, and of an evening she doesn't set by and gossip."

He topped out on a rise and drew up to study the country, and me beside him. "You got to figure most of these folks come from small towns where they never knew much aside from their families, their gossip and their church. It doesn't seem right to them that a decent woman would find time to learn Sioux."

Burt studied the country. "Time was, any stranger was an enemy, and if anybody came around who wasn't one of yours, you killed him. I've seen wolves jump on a wolf that was white or different somehow—seems like folks and animals fear anything that's unusual."

We circled, and I staked out my horses and took the oxen to the herd. By the time ma had her grub-box lid down, I was fixing at a fire when here come Mr. Buchanan, Mr. and Mrs. White and some other folks, including that Webb.

"Ma'am"—Mr. Buchanan was mighty abrupt—"we figure we ought to know what you said to those Sioux. We want to know why they turned off just because you went out there."

"Does it matter?"

Mr. Buchanan's face stiffened up. "We think it does. There's some think you might be an Indian your own self."

"And if I am?" Ma was amused. "Just what is it you have in mind, Mr. Buchanan?"

"We don't want no Injuns in this outfit!" Mr. White shouted.

"How does it come you can talk that language?" Mrs. White demanded. "Even Tryon Burt can't talk it."

"I figure maybe you want us to keep goin' because there's a trap up ahead!" White declared.

I never realized folks could be so mean, but there they were facing ma like they hated her, like those witch-hunters ma told me about back in Salem. It didn't seem right that ma, who they didn't like, had saved them from an Indian attack, and the fact that she talked Sioux like any Indian bothered them.

"As it happens," ma said, "I am not an Indian, although I should not be ashamed of it if I were. They have many admirable qualities. However, you need worry yourselves no longer, as we part company in the morning. I have no desire to travel further with you—*gentlemen.*"

Mr. Buchanan's face got all angry, and he started up to say something mean. Nobody was about to speak rough to ma with me standing by, so I just picked up that ol' rifle and jacked a shell into the chamber. "Mr. Buchanan, this here's my ma, and she's a lady, so you just be careful what words you use."

"Put down that rifle, you young fool!" he shouted at me.

"Mr. Buchanan, I may be little and may be a fool, but this here rifle doesn't care who pulls its trigger."

He looked like he was going to have a stroke, but he just turned sharp around and walked away, all stiff in the back.

"Ma'am," Webb said, "you've no cause to like me much, but you've shown more brains than that passel o' fools. If you'll be so kind, me and my boy would like to trail along with you."

"I like a man who speaks his mind, Mr. Webb. I would consider it an honor to have your company."

Tryon Burt looked quizzically at ma. "Why, now, seems to me this is a time for a man to make up his mind, and I'd like to be included along with Webb."

"Mr. Burt," ma said, "for your own information, I grew up among Sioux children in Minnesota. They were my playmates."

Come daylight our wagon pulled off to one side, pointing northwest at the mountains, and Mr. Buchanan led off to the west. Webb followed ma's wagon, and I sat watching Mr. Buchanan's eyes get angrier as John Sampson, Neely Stuart, the two Shafter wagons and Tom Croft all fell in behind us.

Tryon Burt had been talking to Mr. Buchanan, but he left off and trotted his horse over to where I sat my horse. Mr. Buchanan looked mighty sullen when he saw half his wagon train gone and with it a lot of his importance as captain.

Two days and nearly forty miles further and we topped out on a rise and paused to let the oxen take a blow. A long valley lay across our route, with mountains beyond it, and tall grass wet with rain, and a flat bench on the mountainside seen through a gray veil of a light shower falling. There was that bench, with the white trunks of aspen on the mountainside beyond it looking like ranks of slim soldiers guarding the bench against the storms.

"Ma," I said.

"All right, Bud," she said quietly, "we've come home."

And I started up the oxen and drove down into the valley where I was to become a man.

GET OUT OF TOWN

Ma said for me to ride into town and hire a man to help with the cows. More than likely she figured I'd hire Johnny Loftus or Ed Shifrin, but I had no liking for either of them. Johnny used to wink and call ma "that widder woman" and Ed, he worked no harder than he had to. Man I hired I'd never seen before.

He wasn't much to look at, first off. He was smaller than Johnny Loftus by twenty pound, and Johnny was only a mite more than half of Ed Shifrin, and this stranger was older than either. Fact is, he was pushing forty, but he had a hard, grainy look that made me figure he'd been up the creek and over the mountain.

He wouldn't weigh over a hundred and forty pounds soaking wet, which he wasn't likely to be in this country, and his face was narrow and dark with black eyes that sized you up careful-like before he spoke. He was a-settin' on the platform down to the depot with his saddle and a war bag that looked mighty empty like he was shy of clothes. He was not saying I, yes, or no to anybody when I rode up to town on that buckskin pa gave me before he was shot down in the street.

Pa let me have the pick of the horses for sale in the town corral, and I taken a fancy to a paint filly with a blaze face.

"Son"—pa was hunkered down on his heels watching the horses—"that filly wouldn't carry you over the hill. She looks mighty pert, but what a man wants to find in horses or partners is stayin' quality. He wants a horse he can ride all day and all night that will still be with him at sunup.

"Now you take that buckskin. He's tough and he's got savvy. Horse or men, son, pick 'em tough and with savvy. Don't pay no attention to the showy kind. Pick 'em to last. Pick 'em to go all the way."

Well, I taken the buckskin, and pa was right. Looking at that man setting on the edge of the platform I decided he was the man we wanted. I gave no further thought to Johnny or Ed.

"Mister," I said, "are you rustling work?"

He turned those black eyes on me and studied me right careful. I was pushing fourteen, but I'd been man of the house for nigh three years now. It didn't seem to make no difference to him that I was a wet-eared boy.

"Now I just might be. What work do you have?"

"Ma and me have a little outfit over against the foothills. We figured to roust our cattle out of the canyons and bring 'em down to sell. There's a month of work, maybe more. We'd pay thirty a month and found and if I do say so, ma is the best cook anywheres around."

He looked at me out of those black, careful eyes and he asked me, "You always hire strangers?"

"No, sir. We usually hire Johnny Loftus or Ed Shifrin or one of the loafers around town, but when I saw you I figured to hire you." The way he looked at me was beginning to worry me some.

"Why me?" he asked.

So I told him what pa said when we bought the buckskin, and for the first time he smiled. His eyes warmed and his face crinkled up and laugh wrinkles showed at the corners of his eyes where they must have been sleeping all the time. "Your pa was a right smart man, son. I'd be proud to work for you."

We started for the livery stable to get him a horse to ride out

to the ranch, and Ed Shifrin was in front of the saloon. He
noticed me and then the man who walked beside me.

"Tom," Ed said, "about time your ma started the roundup.
You want I should come out?"

Did me good to tell him, the way he'd loafed on the job and
come in high and mighty over me. "I done hired me a man,
Ed."

Shifrin came down off the walk. "You shouldn't have done
that. The Coopers ain't goin' to like a stranger proddin' around
among their cows." He turned to the man I hired. "Stranger,
you just light a shuck. I'll do the roundin' up."

The man I'd hired didn't seem a mite bothered. "The boy
hired me," he said. "If he don't want me he can fire me."

Ed wasn't inclined to be talked up to. "You're a stranger
hereabouts or you'd know better. There's been range trouble
and the Coopers don't take kindly to strangers among their
stock."

"They'll get used to it," he said, and we walked away up the
street.

About then I started worrying about what I'd done. We'd
tried to avoid trouble. "The Coopers," I told him, "they're the
biggest outfit around here. They sort of run things."

"Who runs your place?"

"Well. Me, sort of. Ma and me. Only she leaves it to me,
because she says a boy without a father has to learn to manage
for himself."

We walked on maybe twenty yards before he said anything,
and then he just said, "Seems to me you've had uncommon
smart folks, boy."

Old Man Taylor brought out the sorrel for us. While the
stranger was saddling up and I sat there enjoying the warm
sunshine and the barn smells of horses and hay and leather,
Old Man Taylor came to where I sat the saddle and he asked
me low-voiced, "Where'd you find him?"

"Down to the depot. He was rustling work and I was looking
for a man."

Old Man Taylor was a man noted for staying out of trouble,

yet he had been friendly to pa. "Boy, you've hired yourself a man. Now you and your ma get set for fireworks."

What he meant I didn't know, nor did it make any kind of sense to me. My hired man came out with the sorrel and he swung into the saddle and we went back down the street. Only he was wearing chaps now and looked more the rider, but somehow he was different from any cowhand I could remember.

We were almost to the end of the street when the sheriff came out of the saloon, followed by Ed Shifrin. He walked into the street and stopped us.

"Tom"—he was abrupt like always—"your ma isn't going to like you hiring this stranger."

"Ma tells me to hire whom I've a mind to. I hired this man and I wouldn't fire any man without he gives me cause."

Sheriff Ben Russell was a hard old man with cold blue eyes and a brusque, unfriendly way about him, but I noticed he cottoned up to the Coopers. "Boy, this man is just out of prison. You get rid of him."

"I'll not hold it against him. I hired him and if he doesn't stack up, I'll fire him."

My hired hand had sat real quiet up to now. "Sheriff," he said, "you just back up and leave this boy alone. He sizes up like pretty much of a man and it begins to look like he really needs outside help. Seems to me there must be a reason folks want to keep a stranger out of the country."

Sheriff Ben Russell was mad as I'd ever seen him. "You can get yourself right back in jail," he said; "you're headed for it."

My hired man was slow to rile. He looked right back at the sheriff with those cold black eyes and he said, "Sheriff, you don't know who I am or why I was in prison. You recognized this prison-made suit. Before you start shaping up trouble for me, you go tell Pike Cooper to come see me first."

Nobody around our country knew a Cooper called Pike, but it was plain to see the sheriff knew who he meant and was surprised to hear him called so. He said, "Where'd you know Cooper?"

"You tell him. I figure he'll know me."

Seven miles out of town we forded the creek and I showed

him with a sweep of the hand. "Our land begins here and runs back into the hills. Our stock has a way of getting into the canyons this time of the year."

"Seems plenty of good grass down here."

"This here is deeded land," I told him. "Pa, he always said the day of free range was over, so he bought homesteads from several folks who had proved up, and he filed on land himself. These are all grazing claims, but two of them have good water holes and the stock fattens up mighty well."

When we rode into the ranch yard ma came to the door, wiping her hands on her apron. She looked at the new rider and I knew she was surprised not to see Ed or Johnny.

The hired man got down from his saddle and removed his hat. Neither Johnny or Ed had ever done that.

"The boy hired me, ma'am, but if you'd rather I'd not stay I'll ride back to town. You see, I've been in prison."

Ma looked at him for a moment, but all she said was, "Tom does the hiring. I feel he should have the responsibility."

"And rightly so, ma'am." He hesitated ever so little. "My name is Riley, ma'am."

Ma said, "Supper's ready. There's a kettle of hot water for washing."

We washed our hands in the tin basin and while he was drying his hands on the towel, Riley said, "You didn't tell me your ma was so pretty."

"I didn't figure there was reason to," I said, kind of stiff.

He took a quick look at me and then he said, "You're right, boy. It's none of my business." Then after a minute he said, "Only it surprised me."

"She was married when she was shy of sixteen," I said.

Supper was a quiet meal. With a stranger at table there were things we didn't feel up to talking about, and you don't ask questions of a man who has been in jail. We made some polite talk about the lack of rain, and how the water on the ranch was permanent, and when he'd finished eating he said, "Mind if I smoke?"

Reckon that was the first time in a while anybody had asked ma a question like that. Pa, he just took it for granted and other men who came around just lit up and said nothing, but the way ma acted you'd have thought it was every day. She said, "Please do." It sounded right nice, come to think of it.

"You been getting good returns on your cattle?"

"The calf crop has been poor the last two, three years, but Ed and Johnny said it was because there were so many lions in the mountains. You have to expect to lose some to lions."

"Good range," Riley said, "and plenty of water. I'd say you should make out."

When he had gone to the bunkhouse ma started picking up the dishes. "How did you happen to hire him, Tom?"

So I told her about the buckskin and what I thought when I saw this man, and she smiled. "I think you learned your lesson well, Tom. I think he is a good man." And then she added, "He may have been in prison, but he had good upbringing."

Coming from ma there was not much more she could have said. She set great store by proper upbringing.

Awhile after, I told her about the talk with Ed Shifrin and Sheriff Russell, and when I came to the part about Riley telling Russell to tell Cooper to come see him, I could see that worried her. Cooper had some tough hands working for him and we didn't want them around.

Year after pa was killed, some of them tried to court ma, but she put a stop to that right off.

Come daylight just as I was pulling on a boot I heard an ax, and when I looked from behind the curtain I saw it was Riley at the woodpile. Right off I could see he was a hand with an ax, but what surprised me was him doing it at all, because most cowhands resent any but riding work, even digging postholes.

The way it worked out we rode away from the place an hour earlier than I'd ever been able to with Ed or Johnny, and by noon we had hazed seventy head down on the flat, but we were mighty shy of young stuff. Whatever else he was, I'd hired a hand. He was up on pa's bay gelding and he knew how to sit a cutting horse and handle a rope.

Next three days we worked like all getout. Riley was up

early and working late, and I being boss couldn't let him best
me, but working with him was like working with pa, for we
shared around and helped each other and I never did see a
man learn country faster than he did. Time to time he'd top out
on high ground and then he'd set a spell and study the country.
Sometimes he'd ask questions. Mostly, he just looked.

Third day we had built us a hatful of fire for coffee and
shucked the wrappings off the lunches ma fixed. "You said your
pa was killed. How'd it happen?"

"Ma and me didn't see it. Pa had been to the Coopers' on
business and when he got back to town he picked up some
dress goods for ma and a few supplies. He was tying the sack
on the saddle when he had a difficulty with a stranger. The
stranger shot him."

"Was your pa wearing a gun?"

"Yes, sir. Pa always wore a gun, but not to use on no man.
He carried it for varmints or to shoot the horse if he got thrown
and his foot caught in the stirrup."

"You hear that stranger's name?"

"Yes, sir. His name was Cad Miller."

That afternoon we ran into Ed Shifrin and Johnny Loftus.
First time I'd seen them up thataway except when working for
us, but they were coming down the draw just as we put out our
fire.

Riley heard them coming before I did, but he looked around
at the mountainside like he was expecting somebody else. He
looked most careful at the trees and rocks where a man might
take cover.

Both of them were armed, but if Riley had a gun I had seen
no sign of it. He wore that buckskin jacket that hung even with
his belt, but there might have been a gun in his waistband
under the jacket. But I didn't think of guns until later.

"You still around?" Shifrin sounded like he was building
trouble. "I figured you'd be run out before this."

"I like it here." Riley talked pleasant-like. "Pretty country,
nice folks. Not as many cows as a man would expect, but
they're fat."

"What d' you mean by that? Not as many cows as you'd expect?"

"Maybe I should have said calves. Not as many calves as a man would expect, but by the time the roundup is over we'll find what happened to the others."

Shifrin looked over at Johnny. "What about the kid?"

Johnny shrugged. "To hell with the kid."

The way they talked back and forth made no sense to me, but it made sense to Riley. "Was I you," Riley said, "I'd be mighty sure Cooper wants it this way. With the kid, and all."

"What d' you mean by that?"

"Why, it just won't work. There's no way you can make it look right. The kid doesn't carry a gun. You boys don't know your business like you should."

"Maybe you know it better?" Johnny sounded mean.

"Why, I do, at that. Did Sheriff Russell tell Pike what I said?"

"Who's Pike?" Shifrin asked suspiciously.

"Why, Pike Cooper. That's what they used to call him in the old days. He ever tell you how he happened to leave Pike County, Missouri? It's quite a story."

Something about the easy way Riley talked was bothering them. They weren't quite so sure of themselves now.

"And while you're at it," Riley added, "you get him to tell you why he left the Nation."

Neither of them seemed to know what to do next. The fact that Riley seemed to know Cooper bothered them, and Johnny was uneasy. He kept looking at me, and I kept looking right back at him, and that seemed to worry him too.

"You boys tell him that. You also tell him not to send boys to do a man's job."

"What's that mean?" Shifrin was sore and he shaped up like a mighty tough man. At least, he always had. Somehow when they came up against Riley they didn't seem either so big or so tough.

"That means you ride out of here now, and you don't stop riding until you get to Pike Cooper. You tell Pike if he wants a job done he'd better come and do it himself."

Well, they didn't know which way was up. They wanted to be tough and they had tried it, but it didn't seem to faze Riley in the least. They had come expecting trouble and now neither one of them wanted to start it and take a chance on being wrong. Or maybe it was the very fact that Riley was taking it so easy. Both of them figured he must have the difference.

"He'll do it!" Johnny replied angrily. "Cooper will want to do this himself. You'll see."

They rode out of there and when Riley had watched them down the slope without comment he said, "We'd best get back to the ranch, Tom. It's early, but we'd better be in when Cooper comes."

"He won't come. Mr. Cooper never goes anywhere unless he feels like it himself."

"He'll come," Riley said, "although he may send Cad Miller first."

When he said that name I stared right at him. "That was the name of the man who killed my father."

"Riley, what I've seen today, I like. If this comes to a case in court I'd admire to be your lawyer."

"Thank you, but I doubt if it will come to that."

We had a quiet supper. We had come in early from the range, so Riley put in the last hour before sundown tightening a sagging gate. He was a man liked to keep busy.

At supper Riley said to ma, "Thank you, ma'am. I am proud to work for you."

Ma blushed.

Next morning ma came to breakfast all prettied up for town. Only thing she said was, "Your father taught you to stand up for what you believe to be right, and to stand by your own people."

There was quite a crowd in town. Word has a way of getting around and folks had a way of being on the street or in the stores when it looked like excitement, and nobody figured to finish their business until it was over.

We left our rig with Old Man Taylor and he leaned over to

whisper, "You tell that friend of yours Cad Miller's in town."

Ma heard it and she turned sharp around. "What does he look like, Mr. Taylor?"

Taylor hesitated, shifting his feet nervous-like, not wanting to say, or figuring why ma wanted to know. But ma wasn't a woman you could shake off. "I asked a question, Mr. Taylor. I believe you were a friend of my husband's."

"Well, ma'am, I figured so. I figured to be a friend of yours, too."

"And so you are. Now tell me."

So he told her.

It was a warm, still morning. We went down to the hotel, where I waited, and ma went out to buy some women fixin's like she won't buy with a man along.

All the chairs were taken in front of the hotel, so I leaned against the corner of the building next to the alley. Moment later I heard Riley speak from behind my right shoulder. He was right around the corner of the building in the alley.

"Don't turn around, boy. Is Cooper on the street?"

"Not yet, but Cad Miller is in town."

"Tom," he said, "just so you'll know. I was in prison for killing a man who'd killed my brother. Before that, I was a deputy United States marshal." He hesitated. "I just wanted you to know."

Nobody on the street was talking much. A rig clattered along the street and disappeared. The dust settled. A yellow hound ambled across the street headed toward shade. Ma went walking up the other side of the street and just when I was wondering what she was doing over there the Coopers turned into the upper end of the street. The boys were riding on his flanks and the old man was driving a shining new buckboard.

Cooper pulled up in front of the hotel and got down. His boys were swaggering it, like always, both of them grinning in appreciation of the fun.

Cooper stepped up on the walk and took a cigar from his vest pocket and bit off the end. His hard old eyes glinted at me. "Boy, where's that hired man of yours? I understand he was asking for me."

"He leaves town today," Andy Cooper said loudly, "or he'll be carried out."

Cooper put the cigar in his teeth. He struck a match and lifted it to light the cigar and I heard a boot grate on the walk beside me and knew Riley was there. Cooper dropped the match without lighting his cigar. He just stood there staring past me at Riley.

"Lark!" Cooper almost choked over the name. "I didn't know it was you."

"You remember what I told you when I ran you out of the Nation?"

Cooper wasn't seeing anybody but Riley, the man he had called Lark. He wasn't even aware of anything else. And I was staring at him, because I had never seen a big man scared before.

"I told you if you ever crossed my trail again I'd kill you."

"Don't do it, Lark. I've got a family—two boys. I've got a ranch. I've done well."

"This boy had a father."

"Lark, don't do it."

"This boy's father has been dead three or four years. I figure you've been stealing his cows at least two years before that. Say five hundred head."

Cooper never took his eyes off him, and the two boys acted as if they couldn't believe what was happening.

"You write out a bill of sale for five hundred head and I'll sign it for the boy's mother. Then you write out a check for seven thousand dollars and we'll cross the street and cash it together."

"All right."

"And you'll testify that Cad Miller was told to kill this boy's pa."

"I can't do that. I won't do it."

"Pike," Riley said patiently, "you might beat a court trial, but you know mighty well you ain't going to beat me. Now my gun's around the corner on my saddle. Don't make me go get it."

Cooper looked like a man who was going to be sick. He looked like a school kid caught cheating. I figured whatever he knew about Riley scared him bad enough so he didn't want any argument. And that talk about a gun on the saddle—why, that might be just talk. A man couldn't see what Riley was packing in his waistband.

"All right," Cooper said. His voice was so low you could scarce hear it.

"Pa!" Andy grabbed his arm. "What are you sayin'?"

"Shut up, you young fool! Shut up, I say!"

"Cad Miller's in town," Riley continued; "you get him out here on the street."

"He won't have to." It was ma's voice.

The crowd moved back and Cad Miller came through with ma right behind him, and trust ma to have the difference. She had a double-barreled shotgun, and she wasn't holding that shotgun for fun. One time I'd seen her use it on a mountain lion right in the door yard. She near cut that lion in two.

Sheriff Ben Russell wasn't liking it very much, but there was nothing he could do but take his prisoner. Once Cooper showed yellow, those two boys of his weren't about to make anything of it, and any man who knew our town knew Cooper was through around here after this.

Back at home I said, "Cooper called you Lark."

"My name is Larkin Riley."

"And you didn't even have a gun!"

"A man has to learn to live without a gun, and against a coward you don't need a gun." He rolled a smoke. "Cooper knew I meant what I said."

"But you'd been in prison yourself."

He sat on the stoop and looked at the backs of his hands. "That was later. Ten or fifteen years ago, what I did would have been the only thing to do. There are laws to handle cases like that, and I had it to learn."

Ma came to the door. "Larkin . . . Tom . . . supper's ready."

We got up and Riley said, "Tom, I think tomorrow we'll work the south range."

"Yes, sir," I said.

BOOTY FOR A BADMAN

When my roan topped out on the ridge, the first thing I saw was that girl. She was far off, but a man riding lonesome country gets so he can pick out anything strange to it, and this girl was standing up straight beside the trail like she was waiting for a stage. Trouble was, nothing but riders or freight wagons used that trail, and seldom.

With fifty pounds of gold riding with me and three days ahead of me, I was skittish of folks. Most times wild country is less trouble than people, no matter how rough the country. And no woman had a right to be standing out there in that empty desert-mountain country.

We Sacketts began carrying rifles as soon as we stood tall enough to keep both ends off the ground.

When I was fourteen I traveled from Cumberland Gap in Tennessee down to the Pine Log Mountains in Georgia, living on cougar meat and branch water, and I killed my own cougars.

Man-grown at fifteen, I hoofed it north and joined up with the Union and fought at Shiloh, and after our outfit was surrendered by a no-account colonel, I was among those exchanged to go north and fight the Sioux in Dakota.

52

At nineteen I saddled our roan and fetched it for the west to try my hand at gold-panning, but I wasn't making out. Seems like everybody in camp was showing color but me, and I was swallowing my belt notch by notch for lack of eating when those four men came to my fire.

Worst of it was, I couldn't offer them. There I was, booting up for a fresh day with my coffeepot on the fire so's people wouldn't know I hadn't even coffee, but all there was in the pot was water. I dearly wanted to offer them, but I was shamed to admit I was fresh out of coffee—three days out, actually. And so hungry that my stomach thought my throat had been cut.

"Tell," Squires suggested, "you've had no luck with mining, so nobody would suspect you of carrying gold. If you rode out of camp today, folks would take it for granted you had called it deep enough and quit. That way you could carry our gold to Hardyville and nobody the wiser."

The four men facing me had taken out the most dust and, knowing about the Coopers, they were worried men. Three of them were family men and that gold meant schooling for their youngsters and homes for their wives and capital for themselves. They were poor, hard-working men, deserving what they had dug up.

Thing was, how to get it past the Coopers?

"We'll give you one hundred dollars," Hodge said, "if you make it through."

With the best of luck it was a five-day ride, which figured out to twenty dollars a day. With such a grubstake I could take out for California or come back with a grubstake.

My belly was as empty as my prospect hole, and it didn't seem like I had much choice. Coopers or no Coopers, it sized up like the fastest hundred dollars I would ever make. It was Bill Squires done it for me, as we'd talked friendly ever since I staked claim on the creek.

Jim Hodge, Willy Mander and Tom Padgett stood there waiting for me to speak up, and finally I said, "I'll do it, of course, and glad of the chance. Only, I am a stranger, and——"

"Squires swears by you," Padgett interrupted, "and even if

we don't know you very well, he's known you and your family. If he says you are honest, that's all there is to it."

"And this is a chance to get you a stake," Squires interrupted. "What can you lose?"

Well, the last two men who rode out of camp with gold were found dead alongside the trail, shot down like you'd shoot a steer; and one of them was Jack Walker, a man I'd known. Neither of them was carrying as much as I'd have.

"Take a pack horse," Squires suggested, "load your gear." He glanced around and lowered his voice, "It seems like somebody here in camp informs the Coopers, but nobody will know about this but us, and all of us have a stake in it."

Later, when the others had gone, Squires said, "Hope you didn't mind my saying I'd known your family. They were willing to trust you if I did, but I wanted them to feel better."

So I packed up and rode off, and in my saddlebags there was fifty pounds of gold, worth around a thousand dollars a pound at the time, and in my pocket I'd a note signed by all four men that I was to have a hundred dollars when the gold was delivered. Never had I seen that much cash money, and since the war I'd not had even ten dollars at one time.

Now, that woman standing down there sized up like trouble aplenty. Pa, he always warned us boys to fight shy of women. "They'll trouble you," pa said. "Love 'em and leave 'em, that's the way. Don't you get tangled up with no female woman. They got more tricks they can do than a monkey on sixty feet of grapevine."

"Don't believe that, Tell," ma would say. "You treat women right. You treat a woman like she was your sister, you hear?"

Pa, he would say, "There's two kinds of women, Tell, good and bad, and believe me, a good woman can cause a man more trouble than a bad one. You fight shy of them."

So I fought shy. Of mountain cats and bears, of muskrat and deer, even of horses and cows I knew a sight, but I wasn't up on womenfolk. Orrin now—he was my brother—he was a fiddler and a singer, and fiddlers and singers have a way with women. At home when strange womenfolk showed up, I'd taken to the hills.

Looked to me like I was fair trapped this time, but I wasn't about to turn and run. Any woman waiting in lonesome country was a woman in trouble. Only I begun to sweat. I'd never been close to no lone woman before.

Worst of it was, there was somebody on my trail. A man like me, riding somewhere, he doesn't only watch the trail ahead, he looks back. Folks get lost because when they start back over a trail they find it looks a sight different facing the other way. When a man travels he should keep sizing up the country, stopping time to time to study his back trail so he recognizes the landmarks.

Looking back, I'd seen dust hanging in the air. And that dust stayed there. It had to be somebody tracking me down, and it could mean it was the Coopers.

Right then I'd much rather have tangled with the Coopers than faced up to that woman down there, but that no-account roan was taking me right to her.

Worst of it was, she was almighty pretty. There was a mite of sunburn on her cheekbones and nose, but despite that, she was a fine-looking girl.

"How do you do?" You'd of thought we were meeting on the streets of Nashville. "I wonder if you could give me a lift to Hardyville?"

My hatbrim was down over my eyes, and I sized up the country around, but there was no sign of a horse she might have ridden to this point, nor any sign of a cabin or camp.

"Why, I reckon so, ma'am." I got down from the saddle, thinking if trouble came I might have to fetch that big Colt in a hurry. "My pack horse is packing light so I can rig that pack saddle so's you can ride it sidesaddle."

"I would be grateful," she said.

First off, it shaped like a trap. Somebody knowing I had gold might have this woman working with them, for it troubled me to guess how she came here. There were a sight of tracks on the ground, but all seemed to be hers. And then I noticed a thin trail of smoke from behind a rock.

"You have a fire?"

"It was quite cold last night."

When she caught my look, she smiled. "Yes, I was here all night." She looked directly at me from those big blue eyes. "And the night before."

"It ain't a likely spot."

She carried herself prim, but she was a bright, quick-to-see girl, and I cottoned to her. The clothes she wore were of fine, store-bought goods like some I'd seen folks wear in some of those northern cities I'd seen as a soldier. Where I came from it was homespun, or buckskin.

"I suppose you wonder what I am doing here?"

"Well, now." I couldn't help grinning. "It did come to my mind. Like I said, it ain't a likely spot."

"You shouldn't say 'ain't.' The word is 'isn't'."

"Thank you, ma'am. I had no schooling, except what ma could give me, and I never learned to talk proper."

"Surely you can read and write?"

"No, ma'am, I surely can't."

"Why, that's awful! Everybody should be able to read. I don't know what I would have done these past months if I could not read. I believe I should have gone insane."

When the saddle was rigged, I helped her up. "Ma'am, I better warn you. There's trouble acoming, so's you'd better have it in mind. It may not be a good thing, me helping you this way. You may get into worse trouble."

We started off, and I looked over my shoulder at her. "Somebody is following after me. I figure it's them Cooper outlaws."

Worst of it was, I had lost time, and here it was coming up to night, and me with a strange girl on my hands. Pa told me women had devious ways of getting to a man, but I never figured one would set out alongside a lonely trail thataway. Especially one as pretty as she was.

Moreover, she was a lady. A body could see she was quality, and she rode there beside me, chin lifted and proud like she was riding the finest thoroughbred at a county fair, or whatever.

"You running from something, ma'am? Not to be disrespectful, ma'am, but out in the desert thisaway it ain't—isn't—just the place a body would expect to find a lady as pretty as you."

"Thank you." Her chin lifted a mite higher. "Yes, I am running away. I am leaving my husband. He is a thoughtless, inconsiderate brute, and he is an Army officer at Fort Whipple."

"He will be mighty sorry to lose you, ma'am. This here is a lonesome country. I don't carry envy for those soldier boys out here, I surely don't."

"Well! It certainly is not a place to bring an officer's bride. I'll declare! How could he think I could live in such a place? With a dirt floor, and all?"

"What did he say when you left?"

"He doesn't know it yet. I had been to Ehrenberg, and when we started back, I just couldn't stand the thought, so when no one was looking, I got out of the Army ambulance I was riding in. I am going to catch the steamer at Hardyville and go home."

When I looked to our back trail, no dust hung in the air, and I knew we were in trouble. If it had been soldiers looking for this girl, they would not have stopped so sudden-like, and it looked to me like they had headed us and laid a trap, so I swung up a draw, heading north instead of west, and slow to raise no dust.

It was a sandy wash, but a thin trail skirted the edge, made by deer or such-like and we held to it. When we had been riding for an hour, I saw dust in the air, hanging up there in a fair cloud about where I had come up to this lady. Again I turned at right angles, heading back the way I had come. Off to the north and west there was a square-topped mesa that was only a part of a long, comb-like range.

"We are followed, ma'am," I said, "and those Coopers are mighty thoughtless folks. I got to keep you out of their hands. First off, we'll run. If that doesn't work, we'll talk or we'll fight, leaving it up to them. You hold with me, ma'am."

"They wouldn't bother me," she said. "I am the wife of an Army officer."

"Most Western men are careful of womenfolk," I agreed, "but don't set no truck by being an officer's wife. The Coopers murdered two Army officers not a week ago. Murdered them, ma'am. They just don't care a mite who you may be. And a woman like you—they don't often see a woman pretty as you."

She rode up closer to me. "I am afraid I didn't realize."

"No, ma'am, most folks don't," I said.

It was still the best part of two days to Hardyville, and nothing much there when we arrived. It was head of navigation on the Colorado, and last I'd seen there were only three or four buildings there, and about that many folks.

Nobody seemed to know how many Coopers there were, but the guesses ran all the way from five to nine. They were said to be renegades from down in the Cherokee nation and mighty mean.

We held to low ground, keeping off skylines, finding a saddle here and there where we could cross over ridges without topping out where we could be seen. It was darkening by then, with long shadows reaching out, and when we came up the eastern flank of that mesa I'd headed for, we rode in deep shadow.

When we found a way around the butte, we took it, and the western slope was all red from the setting sun, and mighty pretty. The wind blew cool there, but I'd found what I was hunting—a place to hole up for the night.

A man hunting a night camp with somebody trailing him has to have things in mind. He wants a place he can get into and out of without skylining himself or showing up plain, and he also wants a place where he can build a fire that cannot be seen, and something to spread out the smoke. And here it was, and by the look of it many an Indian had seen the worth of it before this time.

The falloff from the mesa rim made a steep slope that fell away for maybe five hundred feet. A man could ride a horse down that slope, but it would be sliding half the time on its rump. The wall of the mesa raised up sheer for some three hundred feet, but there at the foot of that cliff and atop the slope was a hollow behind some rocks and brush.

Maybe it was a half-acre of ground with grass in the bottom

and some scraggly cedars at one end. We rode down into that hollow, and I reached up and handed down the lady.

"Ma'am, we'll spend the night here. Talk low and don't let any metal strike metal or start any rock sliding."

"Are they that close?"

"I don't rightly know, ma'am, but we should hope for the best and expect the worst. Pa said that was the way to figure."

When the saddles were off, I climbed out on one of those big rock slabs to study the country. You've got to see country in more than one light to get the lay of it. Shadows tell a lot, and the clear air of early morning or late evening will show up things that are sun-blurred by day. A man scouting country had best size it up of an evening, for shadows will tell him where low ground is, and he can spot the likely passes if only to avoid them.

Pa, who trapped with Bridger and Carson, never lost a chance of teaching us boys how to judge terrain, and the best time was at sundown or sunup with the shadows falling toward you.

When I finished my study, I came down off the rock and cleared a spot of needles and leaves under one of those cedars that sort of arched out toward us. My fire was about the size you could hold in your two hands, for the smaller the fire, the less smoke, and such a fire will heat up just as well if a man wants to cook. And rising up through the branches thataway the smoke would be thinned out so much it could not be seen.

"I'm from Tennessee," I said to her, "and my name is Tell Sackett."

"Oh—I am Christine Mallory, and I was born in Delaware."

"Howdy, Mrs. Mallory. Mostly, the Delawares a man meets out here are Indians. Good trackers and good fighting men."

When I dug out what grub I had, I was ashamed it was so little. It was a mite Squires staked me to before I taken out. The coffee was mostly ground bean and chicory, and all else I had was jerked venison and cold flour.

When the coffee was ready I filled my cup and passed it to her. "Mrs. Mallory, this isn't what you have been used to, but it's all we've got."

She tasted it, and if she hadn't been a lady I think she would have spit, but she swallowed it, and then drank some more. "It's hot," she said, and smiled at me, and I grinned back at her. Truth to tell, that was about all a body could say for it.

"You'd better try some of this jerked venison," I said. "If you hold it in your mouth awhile before you begin to chew, it tastes mighty wholesome. All else I've got is cold flour."

"What?"

"Cold flour—it's a borrowed thing, from the Indians. Only what I have here is white-man style. It's parched corn ground up and mixed with a mite of sugar and cinnamon. You can mix it with water and drink it, and a man can go for miles on it. Mighty nourishing too. Pa was in Montana one time and traveled two weeks on a couple of dry quarts of it."

Last time I got up to scout the country around I caught the gleam of a far-off campfire.

Standing there looking across country and watching the stars come out, I thought of that girl and wondered if I would ever have me a woman like that one, and it wasn't likely. We Sacketts are Welsh, and a proud people, but we never had much in the way of goods. Somehow the Lord's wealth never seemed to gather to us; all we ever had was ourselves and our strength and a will to walk the earth with honesty and pride.

But this girl was running away, and it didn't seem right. She was huddled to the fire, wrapped in one of my blankets when I came down to the fire. Gathering cedar boughs and grass, I made her a bed to one side, but close to the fire.

"The fire smells good," she said.

"That's cedar," I said, "and some creosote brush. Some folks don't like the smell of creosote. Those Spanish men call it *hediondilla*, which means little stinker. Some of the Indians use it for rheumatism."

Nobody said anything for a while, and then I said, "Creosote-brush fires flavor beans—the best ever. You try them sometime, and no beans ever taste the same after."

The fire crackled, and I added a few small, dry sticks and

then said, "It ain't right, leaving him thisaway. He's likely worried to death."

She looked across the fire at me, all stiff and perky. "That is none of your business!"

"Mrs. Mallory, when you saddled yourself on me, you made it my business. Girl who marries a soldier ought to think to live a soldier's life. Strikes me you've no nerve, ma'am, you cut and run because of dirt floors. I'd figure if a girl loved a man it wouldn't make her no mind. You're spoiled, ma'am. You surely are."

She got up, standing real stiff, coming the high and mighty on me. "If you do not want me here, I will go."

"No, you won't. First off, you haven't an idea where you are or which way to go to get there. You'd die of thirst, if that lion didn't get you."

"Lion?"

"Yes, ma'am." I wasn't exactly lying, because somewhere in Arizona there was sure to be a lion prowling. "There's snakes, too, and at night you can't see them until they get stepped on."

She stood there looking unsure of herself, and I kept on with what I had to say. "Woman needs a man out here—needs him bad. But a man needs a woman too. How do you think that man of yours feels now? His wife has shamed him before others, taking on like a girl-baby, running off."

She sat down by the fire, but she looked at me with a chilly expression. "I will thank you to take me to Hardyville. I did not mean to 'saddle' myself on you, as you put it. I will gladly pay you for your trouble."

"Ain't that much money."

"Don't say 'ain't'!" She snapped her eyes at me.

"Thank you, ma'am," I said, "but you better get you some shut-eye. We got to ride fifty miles tomorrow, and I can't be bothered with any tired female. You sit up on that horse tomorrow or I'll dump you in the desert."

"You wouldn't dare!"

"Yes, ma'am, I surely would. And leave you right there, and all your caterwauling wouldn't do you a mite of good. You get some sleep. Come daylight we're taking out of here faster than a scared owl."

Taking up my rifle I went out to scout the country, and setting up there on that rock slab I done my looking and listening. That fire was still aburning, away off yonder, like a star fallen out of the sky.

When I came back, she was lying on the bed I'd made, wrapped in a blanket, already asleep. Seen like that with the firelight on her face she looked like a little girl.

It was way shy of first light when I opened my eyes, and it'd taken me only a minute or two to throw the saddles on those broncs. Then I fixed that pack saddle for her to ride. My outfit was skimpy, so it wasn't much extra weight, carrying her.

When I had coffee going, I stirred her awake with a touch on the shoulder, and her eyes flared open and she was like to scream when she saw me, not that I'd blame her. In my sock feet I stand six-three, and I run to shoulders and hands, with high cheekbones and a wedge face that sun had made dark as any Indian. With no shave and little sleep I must have looked a frightening thing.

"You better eat a little," I said. "You got five minutes."

We rode out of there with the stars still in the sky, and I was pleasant over seeing no fire over yonder where it had been the night before.

It was just shy of noon, with the sun hot in the sky, when we crossed a low saddle and started out across a plain dotted with Joshua trees—named by the Mormons who thought they looked like Joshua lifting his arms to Heaven.

We came down across that country, and there had been no dust in the sky all morning, but of a sudden four men rode up out of a draw, and it was the Coopers. Their description had been talked around enough.

"Howdy, Coopers! You hunting something?"

They looked at Christine Mallory and then at me. "We're looking for you," one said, "and that gold, but we'll take the lady, too, sort of a bonus-like."

Like I said, when you've quit running, you can talk or you can fight, and times like this I run long on talk.

"You'll take nothing," I said. "You are talking to Tell Sackett— William Tell Sackett, to be exact, as my pa favored William Tell in his thinking. We Sacketts hail from the Cumberland Gap in Tennessee, and pa always taught us never to give up nothing without a fight. Specially money or a woman.

"Now," I continued on before they could interrupt, "back to home, folks used to say I wasn't much for fiddling or singing, and my feet was too big for dancing, but along come fighting time, I'd be around.

"Couple of you boys are wearing brass buttons. I figure a forty-four slug would drive one of those buttons so deep into your belly a doc would have to get him a search warrant to find it."

My horse was stepping around kind of uneasy-like, and I was making a show of holding him in.

"Anyway," I said, "this here is General James Whitfield Mallory's wife, and if you so much as lay a hand to her, this territory wouldn't be big enough to hold you. He's the kind to turn out the whole frontier Army just to hunt you."

My horse gave a quick sidestep about then, and when he swung his left side to them, I used the moment to fetch out my gun, and when the roan stopped sidestepping, I had that big Colt looking at them.

Pa, he set me to practicing getting a gun out as soon as the end of my holster quit cutting a furrow in the ground when I walked. Pa said to me, "Son, you ever need that gun, you'll need it in your fist, not in no holster."

They were surprised when they saw that gun staring them down, and this George Cooper was mad clean through. "That ain't going to cut no ice," he said. "We want you, we'll take you."

"One thing about this country," I said, "a man's got a right to his opinion. Case like this here, if you're wrong, you don't get a chance to try it over. Any time you want to give it a try," I said, "you just unlimber and have at it."

Nobody had anything to say, none of those Coopers looking

anything but mad right about then, so I kept on, figuring when we were talking we weren't fighting.

"I got me a bet, Coopers; I got me a bet says I can kill three of you before you clear leather—and that last man better make it a quick shot or I'll make it four."

"You talk a good fight," George Cooper said.

"You can call my hand. You got the right. One thing I promise, if I don't kill you dead with my first shots, I'll leave you lay for the buzzards and the sun."

Those Coopers didn't like it much, but my roan was standing rock still now that I'd quit nudging him with my spur, and at that range a man wasn't likely to miss very often. And it's a fact that nobody wants to die very much.

"If she's Mallory's wife, what's she doing with you?"

"She was headed for Whipple," I said, "and she turned sick, and the doc said she should go back to Ehrenberg. They asked me to take her there. Served with the general during the war," I added. "He knows me well."

"I never heard of no General Mallory," George Cooper said.

"You never heard of *General James Whitfield Mallory*?" By now I believed in him my own self. "He was aide to General Grant! Same class at the Point with Phil Sheridan and Jeb Stuart. Fact is, they are talking of making him governor of the territory just to wipe out outlaws and such.

"Begging the lady's pardon, but he's noted for being a mighty mean man—strict. And smart? He's slicker than a black snake on a wet-clay sidehill. Last thing you want to do is get him riled.

"Lady here was telling me if he is made territorial governor he plans to recruit a special police force from among the Apache. He figures if those Apaches hate white men they might as well turn it to use tracking down outlaws—and he doesn't say anything about them bringing anybody back."

"That's not human!" George Cooper protested.

"That's the general for you. He's that kind." Now that trusty Colt had stayed right there in my fist, and so I said, "Now, we'll ride on."

Motioning her on ahead, I rode after her, but believe me, I

sat sidewise in my saddle with that Colt ready for a quick shot. The last I could see they were still asetting there, arguing.

Most talking I'd done since leaving Tennessee, and the most lying I'd done since who flung the chunk.

We fetched up to Hardyville about sundown on the second day, and the first person I saw when we rode up to the store was Bill Squires.

"Bill," I said, "the Coopers were ahunting me. Only way they could have known I had that gold was if you told them. Somebody had to ride out to tell them, and somebody would want to be on hand to divvy up.

"Now," I said, "if you want to call me a liar, I'll take this lady inside and I'll come right back. But you hear this: they didn't get one speck of this gold, and neither are you."

"I panned my share of that gold!" He was looking mighty bleak.

"So you did, but yours wasn't enough; you had to try for all of it. A month or so back Jack Walker left camp and was drygulched. I plan to send your gold to his widow and family, and you can save your objections to that until I come out."

So I went inside with Christine Mallory, and there were two or three fresh Army officers right off the boat waiting to go to Fort Whipple.

"My husband is not a general," she said then, "and his name is Robert Mallory."

"I know that, Mrs. Mallory. Your husband is Second Lieutenant Robert Mallory, and he's greener than meadow grass. Month or so back he came out and ordered me to get my horse off the parade ground at Whipple. Mighty stiff-necked he was too.

"Ma'am, you haven't got you a man there, you've got a boy, but a boy sound in wind and limb; and two or three years on the frontier will give you a man you can be proud of. But if you run off now the chances are he will resign his commission and run after you, and you'll have a boy for a husband as long as you live.

"You stay with him, you hear? You ain't much account, either, but give you seasoning and you will be. Fact is, if you'd been a woman back there on that trail I might have been less of the gentleman, but you haven't grown up to a man yet."

She had the prettiest blue eyes you ever saw, and she looked straight at me. She was mad, but she was honest, and behind those blue eyes she had a grain of sense.

"You may be right," she admitted, "although I'd rather slap your face than agree. After what I have been through these past few days, that dirt floor would look very good indeed."

"Ma'am, when my time comes to marry, I hope I find a woman as pretty as you—and with as much backbone."

Leaving her talking to those officers, I went to the counter with my gold and checked it in with Hardy in the names of those to whom it was credited, to Jim Hodge, Willy Mander, Tom Padgett—and to Mrs. Jack Walker, whose address I supplied.

"And I've got a hundred dollars coming," I said.

Hardy paid it to me, and I put it in my pocket. More money than I'd seen since the coon went up the tree.

Then I went outside like I'd promised, and Bill Squires surprised me. He was sure enough waiting.

He shot at me and missed. I shot at him and didn't.

THE GIFT OF COCHISE

Tense, and white to the lips, Angie Lowe stood in the door of her cabin with a double-barreled shotgun in her hands. Beside the door was a Winchester '73, and on the table inside the house were two Walker Colts.

Facing the cabin were twelve Apaches on ragged calico ponies, and one of the Indians had lifted his hand, palm outward. The Apache sitting the white-splashed bay pony was Cochise.

Beside Angie were her seven-year-old son Jimmy and her five-year-old daughter Jane.

Cochise sat his pony in silence; his black, unreadable eyes studied the woman, the children, the cabin, and the small garden. He looked at the two ponies in the corral and the three cows. His eyes strayed to the small stack of hay cut from the meadow, and to the few steers farther up the canyon.

Three times the warriors of Cochise had attacked this solitary cabin and three times they had been turned back. In all, they had lost seven men, and three had been wounded. Four ponies had been killed. His braves reported that there was no man in the house, only a woman and two children, so Cochise had come to see for himself this woman who was so certain a shot with a rifle and who killed his fighting men.

These were some of the same fighting men who had outfought, outguessed and outrun the finest American army on record, an army outnumbering the Apaches by a hundred to one. Yet a lone woman with two small children had fought them off, and the woman was scarcely more than a girl. And she was prepared to fight now. There was a glint of admiration in the old eyes that appraised her. The Apache was a fighting man, and he respected fighting blood.

"Where is your man?"

"He has gone to El Paso." Angie's voice was steady, but she was frightened as she had never been before. She recognized Cochise from descriptions, and she knew that if he decided to kill or capture her it would be done. Until now, the sporadic attacks she had fought off had been those of casual bands of warriors who raided her in passing.

"He has been gone a long time. How long?"

Angie hesitated, but it was not in her to lie. "He has been gone four months."

Cochise considered that. No one but a fool would leave such a woman, or such fine children. Only one thing could have prevented his return. "Your man is dead," he said.

Angie waited, her heart pounding with heavy, measured beats. She had guessed long ago that Ed had been killed but the way Cochise spoke did not imply that Apaches had killed him, only that he must be dead or he would have returned.

"You fight well," Cochise said. "You have killed my young men."

"Your young men attacked me." She hesitated, then added, "They stole my horses."

"Your man is gone. Why do you not leave?"

Angie looked at him with surprise. "Leave? Why, this is my home. This land is mine. This spring is mine. I shall not leave."

"This was an Apache spring," Cochise reminded her reasonably.

"The Apache lives in the mountains," Angie replied. "He

does not need this spring. I have two children, and I do need it."

"But when the Apache comes this way, where shall he drink? His throat is dry and you keep him from water."

The very fact that Cochise was willing to talk raised her hopes. There had been a time when the Apache made no war on the white man. "Cochise speaks with a forked tongue," she said. "There is water yonder." She gestured toward the hills, where Ed had told her there were springs. "But if the people of Cochise come in peace they may drink at this spring."

The Apache leader smiled faintly. Such a woman would rear a nation of warriors. He nodded at Jimmy. "The small one— does he also shoot?"

"He does," Angie said proudly, "and well, too!" She pointed to an upthrust leaf of prickly pear. "Show them, Jimmy."

The prickly pear was an easy two hundred yards away, and the Winchester was long and heavy, but he lifted it eagerly and steadied it against the doorjamb as his father had taught him, held his sight an instant, then fired. The bud on top of the prickly pear disintegrated.

There were grunts of appreciation from the dark-faced warriors. Cochise chuckled. "The little warrior shoots well. It is well you have no man. You might raise an army of little warriors to fight my people."

"I have no wish to fight your people," Angie said quietly. "Your people have your ways, and I have mine. I live in peace when I am left in peace. I did not think," she added with dignity, "that the great Cochise made war on women!"

The Apache looked at her, then turned his pony away. "My people will trouble you no longer," he said. "You are the mother of a strong son."

"What about my two ponies?" she called after him. "Your young men took them from me."

Cochise did not turn or look back, and the little cavalcade of riders followed him away. Angie stepped back into the cabin and closed the door. Then she sat down abruptly, her face white, the muscles in her legs trembling.

When morning came, she went cautiously to the spring for

water. Her ponies were back in the corral. They had been returned during the night.

Slowly, the days drew on. Angie broke a small piece of the meadow and planted it. Alone, she cut hay in the meadow and built another stack. She saw Indians several times, but they did not bother her. One morning, when she opened her door, a quarter of antelope lay on the step, but no Indian was in sight. Several times, during the weeks that followed, she saw moccasin tracks near the spring.

Once, going out at daybreak, she saw an Indian girl dipping water from the spring. Angie called to her, and the girl turned quickly, facing her. Angie walked toward her, offering a bright red silk ribbon. Pleased, the Apache girl left.

And the following morning there was another quarter of antelope on her step—but she saw no Indian.

Ed Lowe had built the cabin in West Dog Canyon in the spring of 1871, but it was Angie who chose the spot, not Ed. In Santa Fe they would have told you that Ed Lowe was good-looking, shiftless and agreeable. He was, also, unfortunately handy with a pistol.

Angie's father had come from County Mayo to New York and from New York to the Mississippi, where he became a tough, brawling river boatman. In New Orleans, he met a beautiful Cajun girl and married her. Together, they started west for Santa Fe, and Angie was born en route. Both parents died of cholera when Angie was fourteen. She lived with an Irish family for the following three years, then married Ed Lowe when she was seventeen.

Santa Fe was not good for Ed, and Angie kept after him until they started south. It was Apache country, but they kept on until they reached the old Spanish ruin in West Dog. Here there were grass, water, and shelter from the wind.

There was fuel, and there were piñons and game. And Angie, with an Irish eye for the land, saw that it would grow crops.

The house itself was built on the ruins of the old Spanish building, using the thick walls and the floor. The location had been admirably chosen for defense. The house was built in a corner of the cliff, under the sheltering overhang, so that approach was possible from only two directions, both covered by an easy field of fire from the door and windows.

For seven months, Ed worked hard and steadily. He put in the first crop, he built the house, and proved himself a handy man with tools. He repaired the old plow they had bought, cleaned out the spring, and paved and walled it with slabs of stone. If he was lonely for the carefree companions of Santa Fe, he gave no indication of it. Provisions were low, and when he finally started off to the south, Angie watched him go with an ache in her heart.

She did not know whether she loved Ed. The first flush of enthusiasm had passed, and Ed Lowe had proved something less than she had believed. But he had tried, she admitted. And it had not been easy for him. He was an amiable soul, given to whittling and idle talk, all of which he missed in the loneliness of the Apache country. And when he rode away, she had no idea whether she would ever see him again. She never did.

Santa Fe was far and away to the north, but the growing village of El Paso was less than a hundred miles to the west, and it was there Ed Lowe rode for supplies and seed.

He had several drinks—his first in months—in one of the saloons. As the liquor warmed his stomach, Ed Lowe looked around agreeably. For a moment, his eyes clouded with worry as he thought of his wife and children back in Apache country, but it was not in Ed Lowe to worry for long. He had another drink and leaned on the bar, talking to the bartender. All Ed had ever asked of life was enough to eat, a horse to ride, an occasional drink, and companions to talk with. Not that he had anything important to say. He just liked to talk.

Suddenly a chair grated on the floor, and Ed turned. A lean, powerful man with a shock of uncut black hair and a torn, weather-faded shirt stood at bay. Facing him across the table were three hard-faced young men, obviously brothers.

Ches Lane did not notice Ed Lowe watching from the bar.

He had eyes only for the men facing him. "You done that deliberate!" The statement was a challenge.

The broad-chested man on the left grinned through broken teeth. "That's right, Ches. I done it deliberate. You killed Dan Tolliver on the Brazos."

"He made the quarrel." Comprehension came to Ches. He was boxed, and by three of the fighting, blood-hungry Tollivers.

"Don't make no difference," the broad-chested Tolliver said. " 'Who sheds a Tolliver's blood, by a Tolliver's hand must die!' "

Ed Lowe moved suddenly from the bar. "Three to one is long odds," he said, his voice low and friendly. "If the gent in the corner is willin', I'll side him."

Two Tollivers turned toward him. Ed Lowe was smiling easily, his hand hovering near his gun. "You stay out of this!" one of the brothers said harshly.

"I'm in," Ed replied. "Why don't you boys light a shuck?"

"No, by—!" The man's hand dropped for his gun, and the room thundered with sound.

Ed was smiling easily, unworried as always. His gun flashed up. He felt it leap in his hand, saw the nearest Tolliver smashed back, and he shot him again as he dropped. He had only time to see Ches Lane with two guns out and another Tolliver down when something struck him through the stomach and he stepped back against the bar, suddenly sick.

The sound stopped, and the room was quiet, and there was the acrid smell of powder smoke. Three Tollivers were down and dead, and Ed Lowe was dying. Ches Lane crossed to him.

"We got 'em," Ed said, "we sure did. But they got me."

Suddenly his face changed. "Oh, Lord in heaven, what'll Angie do?" And then he crumpled over on the floor and lay still, the blood staining his shirt and mingling with the sawdust.

Stiff-faced, Ches looked up. "Who was Angie?" he asked.

"His wife," the bartender told him. "She's up northeast somewhere, in Apache country. He was tellin' me about her. Two kids, too."

Ches Lane stared down at the crumpled, used-up body of Ed Lowe. The man had saved his life.

One he could have beaten, two he might have beaten; three would have killed him. Ed Lowe, stepping in when he did, had saved the life of Ches Lane.

"He didn't say where?"

"No."

Ches Lane shoved his hat back on his head. "What's north-east of here?"

The bartender rested his hands on the bar. "Cochise," he said. . . .

For more than three months, whenever he could rustle the grub, Ches Lane quartered the country over and back. The trouble was, he had no lead to the location of Ed Lowe's homestead. An examination of Ed's horse revealed nothing. Lowe had bought seed and ammunition, and the seed indicated a good water supply, and the ammunition implied trouble. But in that country there was always trouble.

A man had died to save his life, and Ches Lane had a deep sense of obligation. Somewhere that wife waited, if she was still alive, and it was up to him to find her and look out for her. He rode northeast, cutting for sign, but found none. Sandstorms had wiped out any hope of back-trailing Lowe. Actually, West Dog Canyon was more east than north, but this he had no way of knowing.

North he went, skirting the rugged San Andreas Mountains. Heat baked him hot, dry winds parched his skin. His hair grew dry and stiff and alkali-whitened. He rode north, and soon the Apaches knew of him. He fought them at a lonely water hole, and he fought them on the run. They killed his horse, and he switched his saddle to the spare and rode on. They cornered him in the rocks, and he killed two of them and escaped by night.

They trailed him through the White Sands, and he left two more for dead. He fought fiercely and bitterly, and would not be turned from his quest. He turned east through the lava beds and still more east to the Pecos. He saw only two white men, and neither knew of a white woman.

The bearded man laughed harshly. "A woman alone? She wouldn't last a month! By now the Apaches got her, or she's dead. Don't be a fool! Leave this country before you die here."

Lean, wind-whipped and savage, Ches Lane pushed on. The Mescaleros cornered him in Rawhide Draw and he fought them to a standstill. Grimly, the Apaches clung to his trail.

The sheer determination of the man fascinated them. Bred and born in a rugged and lonely land, the Apaches knew the difficulties of survival; they knew how a man could live, how he must live. Even as they tried to kill this man, they loved him, for he was one of their own.

Lane's jeans grew ragged. Two bullet holes were added to the old black hat. The slicker was torn; the saddle, so carefully kept until now, was scratched by gravel and brush. At night he cleaned his guns and by day he scouted the trails. Three times he found lonely ranch houses burned to the ground, the buzzard- and coyote-stripped bones of their owners lying nearby.

Once he found a covered wagon, its canvas flopping in the wind, a man lying sprawled on the seat with a pistol near his hand. He was dead and his wife was dead, and their canteens rattled like empty skulls.

Leaner every day, Ches Lane pushed on. He camped one night in a canyon near some white oaks. He heard a hoof click on stone and he backed away from his tiny fire, gun in hand.

The riders were white men, and there were two of them. Joe Tompkins and Wiley Lynn were headed west, and Ches Lane could have guessed why. They were men he had known before, and he told them what he was doing.

Lynn chuckled. He was a thin-faced man with lank yellow hair and dirty fingers. "Seems a mighty strange way to get a woman. There's some as comes easier."

"This ain't for fun," Ches replied shortly. "I got to find her."

Tompkins stared at him. "Ches, you're crazy! That gent declared himself in of his own wish and desire. Far's that goes, the gal's dead. No woman could last this long in Apache country."

At daylight, the two men headed west, and Ches Lane turned south.

Antelope and deer are curious creatures, often led to their

death by curiosity. The longhorn, soon going wild on the plains, acquires the same characteristic. He is essentially curious. Any new thing or strange action will bring his head up and his ears alert. Often a longhorn, like a deer, can be lured within a stone's throw by some queer antic, by a handkerchief waving, by a man under a hide, by a man on foot.

This character of the wild things holds true of the Indian. The lonely rider who fought so desperately and knew the desert so well soon became a subject of gossip among the Apaches. Over the fires of many a rancheria they discussed this strange rider who seemed to be going nowhere, but always riding, like a lean wolf dog on a trail. He rode across the mesas and down the canyons; he studied sign at every water hole; he looked long from every ridge. It was obvious to the Indians that he searched for something—but what?

Cochise had come again to the cabin in West Dog Canyon. "Little warrior too small," he said, "too small for hunt. You join my people. Take Apache for man."

"No." Angie shook her head. "Apache ways are good for the Apache, and the white man's ways are good for white men— and women."

They rode away and said no more, but that night, as she had on many other nights after the children were asleep, Angie cried. She wept silently, her head pillowed on her arms. She was as pretty as ever, but her face was thin, showing the worry and struggle of the months gone by, the weeks and months without hope.

The crops were small but good. Little Jimmy worked beside her. At night, Angie sat alone on the steps and watched the shadows gather down the long canyon, listening to the coyotes yapping from the rim of the Guadalupes, hearing the horses blowing in the corral. She watched, still hopeful, but now she knew that Cochise was right: Ed would not return.

But even if she had been ready to give up this, the first home she had known, there could be no escape. Here she was protected by Cochise. Other Apaches from other tribes would not so willingly grant her peace.

At daylight she was up. The morning air was bright and balmy, but soon it would be hot again. Jimmy went to the spring for water, and when breakfast was over, the children played while Angie sat in the shade of a huge old cottonwood and sewed. It was a Sunday, warm and lovely. From time to time, she lifted her eyes to look down the canyon, half-smiling at her own foolishness.

The hard-packed earth of the yard was swept clean of dust; the pans hanging on the kitchen wall were neat and shining. The children's hair had been clipped, and there was a small bouquet on the kitchen table.

After a while, Angie put aside her sewing and changed her dress. She did her hair carefully, and then, looking in her mirror, she reflected with sudden pain that she *was* pretty, and that she was only a girl.

Resolutely, she turned from the mirror and, taking up her Bible, went back to the seat under the cottonwood. The children left their playing and came to her, for this was a Sunday ritual, their only one. Opening the Bible, she read slowly,

". . . though I walk through the valley of the shadow of death, I will fear no evil; for thou art with me; thy rod and thy staff, they comfort me. Thou preparest a table before me in the presence of mine enemies; thou . . . ."

"Mommy." Jimmy tugged at her sleeve. "Look!"

Ches Lane had reached a narrow canyon by midafternoon and decided to make camp. There was small possibility he would find another such spot, and he was dead tired, his muscles sodden with fatigue. The canyon was one of those unexpected gashes in the cap rock that gave no indication of its presence until you came right on it. After some searching, Ches found a route to the bottom and made camp under a wind-hollowed overhang. There was water, and there was a small patch of grass.

After his horse had a drink and a roll on the ground, it began cropping eagerly at the rich, green grass, and Ches built a smokeless fire of ancient driftwood in the canyon bottom. It was his first hot meal in days, and when he had finished he put out his fire, rolled a smoke, and leaned back contentedly.

Before darkness settled, he climbed to the rim and looked over the country. The sun had gone down, and the shadows were growing long. After a half hour of study, he decided there was no living thing within miles, except for the usual desert life. Returning to the bottom, he moved his horse to fresh grass, then rolled in his blanket. For the first time in a month, he slept without fear.

He woke up suddenly in the broad daylight. The horse was listening to something, his head up. Swiftly, Ches went to the horse and led it back under the overhang. Then he drew on his boots, rolled his blankets, and saddled the horse. Still he heard no sound.

Climbing the rim again, he studied the desert and found nothing. Returning to his horse, he mounted up and rode down the canyon toward the flatland beyond. Coming out of the canyon mouth, he rode right into the middle of a war party of more than twenty Apaches—invisible until suddenly they stood up behind rocks, their rifles leveled. And he didn't have a chance.

Swiftly, they bound his wrists to the saddle horn and tied his feet. Only then did he see the man who led the party. It was Cochise.

He was a lean, wiry Indian of past fifty, his black hair streaked with gray, his features strong and clean-cut. He stared at Lane, and there was nothing in his face to reveal what he might be thinking.

Several of the young warriors pushed forward, talking excitedly and waving their arms. Ches Lane understood none of it, but he sat straight in the saddle, his head up, waiting. Then Cochise spoke and the party turned, and, leading his horse, they rode away.

The miles grew long and the sun was hot. He was offered no water and he asked for none. The Indians ignored him. Once a young brave rode near and struck him viciously. Lane made no sound, gave no indication of pain. When they finally stopped, it was beside a huge anthill swarming with big red desert ants.

Roughly, they untied him and jerked him from his horse. He dug in his heels and shouted at them in Spanish: "The Apaches are women! They tie me to the ants because they are afraid to fight me!"

An Indian struck him, and Ches glared at the man. If he must die, he would show them how it should be done. Yet he knew the unpredictable nature of the Indian, of his great respect for courage.

"Give me a knife, and I'll kill any of your warriors!"

They stared at him, and one powerfully built Apache angrily ordered them to get on with it. Cochise spoke, and the big warrior replied angrily.

Ches Lane nodded at the anthill. "Is this the death for a fighting man? I have fought your strong men and beaten them. I have left no trail for them to follow, and for months I have lived among you, and now only by accident have you captured me. Give me a knife," he added grimly, "and I will fight *him!*" He indicated the big, black-faced Apache.

The warrior's cruel mouth hardened, and he struck Ches across the face.

The white man tasted blood and fury. "Woman!" Ches said. "Coyote! You are afraid!" Ches turned on Cochise, as the Indians stood irresolute. "Free my hands and let me fight!" he demanded. "If I win, let me go free."

Cochise said something to the big Indian. Instantly, there was stillness. Then an Apache sprang forward and, with a slash of his knife, freed Lane's hands. Shaking loose the thongs, Ches Lane chafed his wrists to bring back the circulation. An Indian threw a knife at his feet. It was his own bowie knife.

Ches took off his riding boots. In sock feet, his knife gripped low in his hand, its cutting edge up, he looked at the big warrior.

"I promise you nothing," Cochise said in Spanish, "but an honorable death."

The big warrior came at him on cat feet. Warily, Ches circled. He had not only to defeat this Apache but to escape.

He permitted himself a side glance toward his horse. It stood alone. No Indian held it.

The Apache closed swiftly, thrusting wickedly with the knife. Ches, who had learned knife-fighting in the bayou country of Louisiana, turned his hip sharply, and the blade slid past him. He struck swiftly, but the Apache's forward movement deflected the blade, and it failed to penetrate. However, as it swept up between the Indian's body and arm, it cut a deep gash in the warrior's left armpit.

The Indian sprang again, like a clawing cat, streaming blood. Ches moved aside, but a backhand sweep nicked him, and he felt the sharp bite of the blade. Turning, he paused on the balls of his feet.

He had had no water in hours. His lips were cracked. Yet he sweated now, and the salt of it stung his eyes. He stared into the malevolent black eyes of the Apache, then moved to meet him. The Indian lunged, and Ches sidestepped like a boxer and spun on the ball of his foot.

The sudden sidestep threw the Indian past him, but Ches failed to drive the knife into the Apache's kidney when his foot rolled on a stone. The point left a thin red line across the Indian's back. The Indian was quick. Before Ches could recover his balance, he grasped the white man's knife wrist. Desperately, Ches grabbed for the Indian's knife hand and got the wrist, and they stood there straining, chest to chest.

Seeing his chance, Ches suddenly let his knees buckle, then brought up his knee and fell back, throwing the Apache over his head to the sand. Instantly, he whirled and was on his feet, standing over the Apache. The warrior had lost his knife, and he lay there, staring up, his eyes black with hatred.

Coolly, Ches stepped back, picked up the Indian's knife, and tossed it to him contemptuously. There was a grunt from the watching Indians, and then his antagonist rushed. But loss of blood had weakened the warrior, and Ches stepped in swiftly, struck the blade aside, then thrust the point of his blade hard against the Indian's belly.

Black eyes glared into his without yielding. A thrust, and the man would be disemboweled, but Ches stepped back. "He is a strong man," Ches said in Spanish. "It is enough that I have won."

Deliberately, he walked to his horse and swung into the saddle. He looked around, and every rifle covered him.

So he had gained nothing. He had hoped that mercy might lead to mercy, that the Apache's respect for a fighting man would win his freedom. He had failed. Again they bound him to his horse, but they did not take his knife from him.

When they camped at last, he was given food and drink. He was bound again, and a blanket was thrown over him. At daylight they were again in the saddle. In Spanish he asked where they were taking him, but they gave no indication of hearing. When they stopped again, it was beside a pole corral, near a stone cabin.

When Jimmy spoke, Angie got quickly to her feet. She recognized Cochise with a start of relief, but she saw instantly that this was a war party. And then she saw the prisoner.

Their eyes met and she felt a distinct shock. He was a white man, a big, unshaven man who badly needed both a bath and a haircut, his clothes ragged and bloody. Cochise gestured at the prisoner.

"No take Apache man, you take white man. This man good for hunt, good for fight. He strong warrior. You take 'em."

Flushed and startled, Angie stared at the prisoner and caught a faint glint of humor in his dark eyes.

"Is this here the fate worse than death I hear tell of?" he inquired gently.

"Who are you?" she asked, and was immediately conscious that it was an extremely silly question.

The Apaches had drawn back and were watching curiously. She could do nothing for the present but accept the situation. Obviously they intended to do her a kindness, and it would not do to offend them. If they had not brought this man to her, he might have been killed.

"Name's Ches Lane, ma'am," he said. "Will you untie me? I'd feel a lot safer."

"Of course." Still flustered, she went to him and untied his hands. One Indian said something, and the others chuckled; then, with a whoop, they swung their horses and galloped off down the canyon.

Their departure left her suddenly helpless, the shadowy globe of her loneliness shattered by this utterly strange man standing before her, this big, bearded man brought to her out of the desert.

She smoothed her apron, suddenly pale as she realized what his delivery to her implied. What must he think of her? She turned away quickly. "There's hot water," she said hastily, to prevent his speaking. "Dinner is almost ready."

She walked quickly into the house and stopped before the stove, her mind a blank. She looked around her as if she had suddenly waked up in a strange place. She heard water being poured into the basin by the door, and heard him take Ed's razor. She had never moved the box. To have moved it would—

"Sight of work done here, ma'am."

She hesitated, then turned with determination and stepped into the doorway. "Yes, Ed—"

"You're Angie Lowe."

Surprised, she turned toward him, and recognized his own startled awareness of her. As he shaved, he told her about Ed, and what had happened that day in the saloon.

"He—Ed was like that. He never considered consequences until it was too late."

"Lucky for me he didn't."

He was younger looking with his beard gone. There was a certain quiet dignity in his face. She went back inside and began putting plates on the table. She was conscious that he had moved to the door and was watching her.

"You don't have to stay," she said. "You owe me nothing. Whatever Ed did, he did because he was that kind of person. You aren't responsible."

He did not answer, and when she turned again to the stove, she glanced swiftly at him. He was looking across the valley.

There was a studied deference about him when he moved to a place at the table. The children stared, wide-eyed and silent; it had been so long since a man sat at this table.

Angie could not remember when she had felt like this. She was awkwardly conscious of her hands, which never seemed to be in the right place or doing the right things. She scarcely tasted her food, nor did the children.

Ches Lane had no such inhibitions. For the first time, he realized how hungry he was. After the half-cooked meat of lonely, trailside fires, this was tender and flavored. Hot biscuits, desert honey . . . Suddenly he looked up, embarrassed at his appetite.

"You were really hungry," she said.

"Man can't fix much, out on the trail."

Later, after he'd got his bedroll from his saddle and unrolled it on the hay in the barn, he walked back to the house and sat on the lowest step. The sun was gone, and they watched the cliffs stretch their red shadows across the valley. A quail called plaintively, a mellow sound of twilight.

"You needn't worry about Cochise," she said. "He'll soon be crossing into Mexico."

"I wasn't thinking about Cochise."

That left her with nothing to say, and she listened again to the quail and watched a lone bright star.

"A man could get to like it here," he said quietly.

A MULE FOR SANTA FE

Sell the mules," Hassoldt advised, "you want oxen. Less water for 'em an' their feet flatten out on the prairie country where a mule's dig in. If you get hard up for grub you can always eat an ox."

"If I get that hungry," Scott Miles replied shortly, "I can eat a mule."

Hassoldt was an abrupt man. He turned away now, his irritation plain. "Suit yourself, Miles. But you'll need another mule and I haven't any for sale."

Bitterly, Scott Miles turned away and went out the door. Rain lashed at his face, for outside the building there was neither awning nor boardwalk. Head bowed into the rain, he slopped along toward the Carter house where young Bill was waiting.

Hassoldt wanted those mules badly, and no wonder. There would be a big demand for them in a few months, and nobody had mules like those of Scott Miles. They were well-bred and well-fed, strapping big mules with plenty of power. If he could get them west there would be money in them.

Everywhere he went they advised against the mules. On roads they were fine. On rocks they were all right. But out on the prairie?

Pembroke advised against them, too. However, after much argument he had agreed to accept the wagon in his company if Miles had a full team of six mules. Four, Pembroke insisted, were not enough. Not even, he added, if the mules were big as those of Miles' team.

There were half a dozen people in the hotel when he stepped in. Pembroke was there, a big, fine-looking man with a tawny mustache. He was talking to Bidwell, a substantial farmer from Ohio who had been the first to sign for Pembroke's fast wagon train.

Miles looked around and found Billy. He was talking to a pretty woman with dark red hair who sat in a big, leather-bound chair.

Bill saw him at once. "Pa," he said excitedly, "this is Mrs. Hance."

She looked up and he was immediately uneasy. She had blue eyes, not dark eyes like Mary's had been, and there was a friendliness in them that disturbed him. "Bill's been telling me about you, Mr. Miles. Have you found a mule?"

Glad to be on familiar ground, he shook his head. "Hassoldt won't sell. I'm afraid I'm out of luck." He was absurdly conscious of his battered hat, its brim limp with rain and his unshaven jaws. He wanted to get away from her. Women like this both irritated and disturbed him. She was too neat, too perfectly at ease. He knew what such women were like on the trail, finicky and frightened of bugs and fussing over trifles. Also, and he was frank to admit it to himself, he was a little jealous of Bill's excited interest.

"We'd better go, Bill. Say good-by to Mrs. Hance."

He walked out, red around the ears and conscious that somehow Bill felt he had failed him. It was not necessary for him to have been so abrupt. Just because he looked like a big backwoods farmer was no reason he should act like one.

They lived in the wagon. It was a big new Conestoga, and his tools were all new. He had his plowshare, he'd make the plow when he got there, and he had two rifles and plenty of ammunition. Bill was nine, but already he could shoot, and Scott Miles wanted his son to grow up familiar with weapons. He wanted him to be a good hunter, to use guns with intelligence.

A boy needed two parents, and being an observant man Scott had not failed to notice the wistfulness in Bill's eyes when other children, hurt or imagining a hurt, ran to mother. Bill would never do that with him, he was too proud of being a little man in front of his father. But it wasn't right for the boy.

Farmer Bidwell had a daughter, a pretty, flush-faced girl with corn-silk hair. She had been casting sidelong glances at him ever since their wagon rolled alongside. Tentatively, Scott Miles touched his chin. He had better shave.

He did, and he also trimmed down his mustache. He wore it Spanish style and not like the brush mustaches of Bidwell or so many of the company. He got into a clean shirt then. Bill eyed him critically. "Gettin' all duded up," he said. "You goin' back to see Mrs. Hance?"

"No!" He spoke sharply. "I may go to see Grace Bidwell, later."

"Her?" Bill's contempt was obvious. So obvious that Scott looked at the boy quickly. "She isn't as pretty as Mrs. Hance."

Scott Miles sat down. "Look, Bill," he said, "we're going into a mighty rough country, like I've told you. We won't be in a city. We'll be in the mountains where I'll have to fell trees and trim them for a cabin.

"Now I need a wife, and you need a mother. But just being pretty isn't enough. I've got to have a wife who can cook, who can make her own clothes if need be. A wife who can take the rough going right with me. I need somebody who can help, not hinder."

Bill nodded, but he remained only half convinced. Scott Miles was shouldering into his coat when Bill spoke again. "Pa," he was frowning a little, "if we get a new mother, shouldn't it be somebody we like, too?"

Scott Miles stared into the rain, his face grim. Then he dropped his hand to Bill's shoulder. "Yes, son," he said quietly, "it would have to be somebody we like . . . too."

The rain stopped, but the sun did not come out. Slopping through the rain, Miles made inquiries about mules. Yes, there was an old hard-case downriver who owned a big black mule. The man's name was Simon Gilbride. Sell him? Not a chance! He wouldn't even talk about it. Nevertheless, Scott Miles saddled his bay mare and rode south. As he started out of town he saw Mrs. Hance on the hotel steps. She waved, and he waved back.

He saw something else, too. Something that filled him with grave disquiet. Hassoldt was standing on the steps talking to three rough-looking men from the river. All wore guns. They turned and looked at him as he passed, and Scott had the uncomfortable feeling they had been talking about him.

Gilbride came to the door when Scott arrived. He was a tall, old man with a cold patrician face and the clothes of a farmer. "Sell my mule? Of course not!" And that was final.

It was dusk before Scott returned to the wagon. He was tired and he sagged in the saddle. It was not so much physical weariness, for he was a big man and unusually strong, but the weariness of defeat. Only a few hours remained and there was only one mule in the country the size of his. Of course, wagons were arriving all the time. If he could keep circulating . . .

He pulled up. There was a fire going and Bill was squatted beside it. He was laughing and eating at the same time, and the girl who was cooking was laughing also. "Good!" he muttered. "Grace has finally got to him. Now things will be easier all around."

Only when she straightened from the fire it was not Grace. It was Mrs. Hance.

She smiled, a little frightened. "Oh! I didn't expect you back so soon. I—I was worried about Bill going without his supper."

The food was good. Had a flavor he didn't know, but mighty

good. And Bill was eating as if he hadn't eaten in years. Of course, Bill could digest anything.

"Mr. Miles," she spoke suddenly as if nerved for the effort. "I have a favor to ask. I want to ride in your wagon to Santa Fe."

He blinked. Of all things, this was the least expected. Bill had looked up and Scott could almost feel him listening.

He shook his head. "I am sorry, Mrs. Hance. The answer is no. It is quite impossible."

He walked to the door of the hotel with her, then back to the wagon. Suddenly he decided to check the mules and, nearing them, he was almost positive he saw a shadow move in the darkness near where they were picketed. He waited, his gun ready, but there was no further movement, no sound.

He waited for a long time in silence, seriously worried. Hassoldt wanted mules badly, with a big contract to fill for the government, and he did not impress Miles as a very scrupulous man. In such a place as this there would be thieves, and Hassoldt impressed him as a man likely to stop at nothing to obtain something he wanted.

When he reached the hotel next morning there was no sign of Mrs. Hance. He hesitated, faintly disappointed at not seeing her. Pembroke and Bidwell were together. "Well, Miles," Pembroke was abrupt. "Have you found a mule? I'm sorry, of course, but if you haven't one tomorrow we'll have to make other arrangements."

Wearily Miles walked back to camp, leading the mare. He was walking up to the wagon when the mare whinnied. He looked up. Tied to a wagon wheel was a magnificent sorrel stallion. At least sixteen hands high, it had a white face and three white stockings. After tying the mare, Scott Miles walked admiringly around the stallion. It was one of the finest animals he had ever seen.

Mrs. Hance came out of the trees with Bill. They hung back a little, then walked toward him.

"This," he inquired, "is your horse?"

"You like him?"

"Like him? He's splendid! All my life I've wanted to own just such a horse. Of course," he added quickly, "I could never afford it."

"With your mare it might be very profitable," she assured him quietly. Then she lifted her chin. "Mr. Miles, what would you do for another mule?"

He laughed grimly. "Anything short of murder," he said, "if I got him before tomorrow."

"Even to sharing your wagon with a widow?"

He chuckled. "Even that!"

"Then prepare to have a passenger. I've got a mule!"

He shook his head. "That's impossible. There isn't a mule within miles and miles of here. I've looked."

"I have a mule," she said, "as big as yours. He was sold to me by Simon Gilbride."

Scott Miles sat down, and she explained very quietly. Determined to go to Santa Fe, she had decided the only thing to do was to personally see the old man.

Gilbride, it turned out, had been in her father's command in Mexico. That, a little pleading and a little flattery had done the trick. "So," she said, "I have a mule. I have the only mule. So if you go you take me. What do we do?"

Scott Miles got to his feet and bowed politely. "Mrs. Hance, will you do me the honor of allowing me to escort you to Santa Fe?"

She curtsied gravely, then her eyes filled with mischief. "Mr. Miles," she replied formally, "I was hoping you'd ask!"

Pembroke was in the hotel, seated with Bidwell and several others, shaping last details of the trip.

"Count me in." Scott could scarcely keep the triumph from his tone. "I've got my mule!"

As he explained he saw Bidwell's face stiffen. Pembroke frowned slightly, then shook his head. "It won't do, Miles," he said. "The women would never stand for it. We can't have an unmarried couple sharing a wagon. It just won't do."

"Look," he protested, "I—" Argument was fruitless. The answer was a flat no. Disgusted, angry and desperate, he started back toward the wagon. He was nearing it when he heard a shot, then another. Running, he whipped his pistol from his waistband and broke through the trees to the wagon.

Mrs. Hance stood behind the wagon with a smoking rifle. Her face was white. "They got away," she said bitterly, "they've stolen our mules!" She continued icily, "Have you decided to just stand there or are you going to take Admiral and go after them?"

"Admiral?" He was astonished. "They didn't get him? You mean he was tied here?"

"Behind the wagon," she said shortly. "Now take him and get started!"

"He might be killed," he warned.

Her lips tightened. "Take him! We're in this together!"

It was morning when he realized he was closing in. Admiral was not merely a beautiful horse, but one with speed and bottom. And one of the men was wounded. He had come upon the place where they bathed and dressed his wound at daylight. He had found fragments of a bloody shirt and fresh boot-tracks.

Two hours later he stopped on the edge of a grove and saw them disappearing into a cluster of piñons a half mile away. They had the mules roped together and they were moving more slowly. The wounded man was riding his mare.

He had no illusions about fair play. They would kill on sight. If he survived he must do the same. Studying the terrain, he saw a long draw off on the right that cut into the plain to the south. If he could get into that draw and beat them to the plain . . .

Admiral went down the bank as if mountainbred and on the bottom he stepped out into a run. Despite the long night of riding, the big horse had plenty left. He ran and ran powerfully, ran with eagerness.

At the draw's opening, Scott Miles swung down. Grimly, he checked the heavy pistol he carried. Thrusting it into his waistband, he walked along through the scattered greasewood and piñon until he was near the entrance of the larger draw down which they were coming.

The mules came out of the draw with the men behind them. Scott Miles drew his pistol and stepped from the piñons, but as his foot came down a rock rolled and he lost balance. He fell backwards, seeing the riders grabbing for their guns. He caught himself on his left hand and fired even as a bullet whisked by his face.

He rolled to one knee and fired again. The second shot did not miss. One man lurched in his saddle and there was blood down the back of his head, and then he fell into the dust, his horse stampeding.

The wounded man had disappeared, but the third man leaped his horse at Scott. There was an instant when Scott saw the flaring nostrils of the horse, saw the man lean wide and point the gun straight at his face. And then Scott fired.

The man's body jolted, seeming to lift from the saddle, and was slammed back as the horse leaped over Miles, one hoof missing him by a hair. The rider hit the sand and rolled over. Taking no chances, Miles fired again.

One man left. Sitting on the sand, half-concealed by brush, Miles reloaded the empty chambers. Then he started through the brush, moving carefully.

The wounded man sat on the ground, holding his one good arm aloft. "Don't shoot!" he begged. "I tossed my gun away."

Scott gathered the guns, then the mules and the horses. He left one horse for the wounded man. "You do what you like, but don't cross my trail again. Not ever."

The mules made a nice picture ahead of the big Conestoga wagon, and on the seat Scott Miles sat beside his wife. She was not only a very pretty woman, this Laura Hance Miles, but, as he had discovered, a useful one.

He was, he admitted, very much in love, a richer and more exciting love than he had ever experienced. There would always be a place in his heart for Mary, but this woman was one to walk beside a man, not behind him. She had shown it since the first day they were two together, a team, working toward a common end. It was what he had wanted.

There had been a time, he remembered, when he had believed a man could never get close to a woman like this. But that had been a long time ago.

And Bill had been right. It was necessary to like somebody, too.

ALKALI BASIN

The stage rocked and rolled over the desert road, vainly pursued by a thick cloud of fine white dust. It plunged down a declivity into a dry wash, then swept up the other side and around a hairpin curve at the top, to straighten out on the long dash across the valley.

Price Macomber, vice-president of the Overland Stage Company, was heading west on an inspection tour accompanied by his niece and Pete Judson, the district superintendent. Price, a round man with a round pink face and round rimless spectacles, was holding forth on his pet theme—useless expenditures.

"It has been my experience," he was saying, "that given the slightest excuse each driver and each station operator will come up with a number of items of utterly useless expense, and such items must be eliminated."

He braced himself against the roll of the stage and stared out the window for an instant as if collecting his thoughts. Then his eyes pinned Judson to his seat as a collector pins a butterfly. Judson squirmed, but there was no escape.

"You understand," Macomber continued, "I'm not accusing these men of including items for their own advantage. No doubt at the moment they believe the item essential, yet when viewed logically it usually proves such claims were arrived at without due consideration.

"Take, for example, the ridiculous request of this man Wells, at Alkali Basin. Four times now he has written us demanding we send him blasting powder!

"Now think of that! Blasting powder, of all things! What earthly use would a station agent have for blasting powder? In our reply to his first request, we suggested he submit his reason for wanting it, and he replied that he wished to blast some rocks.

"Were the rocks on the road? No, they were not. They were some seventy yards off the road in the desert. The request was, without doubt, the whimsical notion of an uneducated man at a moment when he was not thinking. By now he no doubt realizes the absurdity of his notion.

"It is such items as this that can be eliminated. And I observed," Macomber added severely, "that you recommended his request be granted. I was surprised, Judson. Needless to say, I was very surprised. We expect better judgment of our district superintendents."

Judson mopped his brow and said nothing. In the past one-hundred-and-ten miles he had learned it was wiser to listen and endure. Price Macomber's voice droned on into the hot, dusty afternoon with no hint of a letup.

The best arguments Judson had offered had been riddled with logic, devastating and inescapable. He would have liked to say that sometimes logic fell short of truth, but lacked the words, and no argument of his could hope to dam the flow of words that poured over the spillway of Price Macomber's lips.

Molly Macomber stared wearily at the desert. Her uncle, so polished, immaculate, and sure of himself, had failed to materialize into the superman he had seemed in Kansas City and St. Louis.

Against the background of the rolling grasslands, she had noticed that his stiff white collar and neat black suit seemed somehow incongruous. Also, among the ragged, stark ridges of the desert, his mouth seemed too prim and precise, his eyes seemed flat and rather foolish. They were like the eyes of a goldfish staring from a bowl at a world it neither understood nor saw clearly.

"Keep the expense down," Macomber was saying, "and the profits will take care of themselves."

Judson stared at the desert and shifted his feet. He felt sorry for Molly, who evidently expected glamour and beauty on this westward trek. He also felt sorry for himself. He took a drink with his stage drivers, and played poker with them. Somehow he had always got results.

He had visited Alkali Basin just once before, and heartily wished he would never have to again. If Wells, keeper of the station there, wanted blasting powder, Judson was for letting him have it. Or anything else, for that matter, including a necklace of silver bells, a Cardinal's hat or even a steamboat— anything to keep him contented.

In the three months before Wells took over the station at Alkali Basin, no fewer than six station agents had attempted the job.

The first man stuck it ten days. It was a lonely post where he had only to change horses for two stages each day, one going east, and one west. After ten days that agent had come to town on the stage and shook his head decisively. "No!" he said violently. "Not for any price! Not even Price Macomber!"

Four days after the next agent took over, the stage rolled into Alkali Basin and found no horses awaiting it. The horses were gone from the corral, and the agent lay across his adobe doorstep shot three times through the body, mutilated and scalped.

Two more men had tried it, one after the other. The Apaches got the first one of these on his second day, and the other man fought them off for a couple of hours, then went to Mexico with two teams of six horses each, and had not been heard from since.

Blasting powder might be somewhat extreme, but in Judson's private, and oft expressed opinion—to everyone but Macomber—

any man who would stick it out for as much as ten days in the
white dust and furnace heat of Alkali Basin, was entitled to
anything he wanted.

The man called Wells had been on the job for two solid
months, and so far, except for the powder, his only request had
been for large quantities of ammunition. He sent in a request
for more by every stage.

Macomber leaned with the sway of the stage as it swung
around a corner of red rock. The movement awakened Molly
who had dozed, made sleepy by the motion of the stage and
the heat. A thin film of dust had settled on her face, her neck
and her hair. Perspiration, extremely unladylike perspiration,
had left streaks on her face.

Her eyes strayed out over the white, dancing heat waves of
the basin's awful expanse. The hot sun reflected from it and
the earth seemed to shimmer, unreal and somehow ghastly.
In the far distance, a column of dust arose and skipped along
over the white desolation like some weird and evil spirit. It was
the only movement.

The stage reached bottom and paused briefly in the partial
shade while the horses gathered breath for the long, bitter run
across the desert bottom, inches deep in alkali.

The pursuing dust cloud caught up with and settled over the
stage and the clothing of the occupants. Even Price Macomber's
dauntless volubility seemed to hesitate and lose itself in space.
He was silent, staring out the window as though totaling a
column of figures. Money saved, no doubt.

As the stage stumbled into movement once more, he glanced
at Judson. "How much further to our stop?"

"Forty miles to a decent place. It's no more than ten miles to
Alkali Basin. We change horses there, but we'd better get food
and water at Green's Creek."

The horses, as though aware of the coming rest, lunged into
the harness and charged at the heat waves.

Six hours earlier, morning had come to Alkali Basin. The
sun, as though worn from its efforts of the previous day,

pushed itself wearily over the jagged ridge in the distance and stabbed with white hot lances at the lonely stone building and the corrals.

Wells, his stubble of beard whitened with alkali, stared through one of the small windows with red-rimmed, sleepless eyes. The Apaches were still there. He couldn't see them, but he knew without seeing. They had been there, devilish in their patience, for eighteen hours now. They were out there in front of him, behind that low parapet of rocks.

He was a big, rawboned man, hairy chested and hard-bitten. His reddish hair was a rumpled, uncombed mass, his shirt was dirty and sweat-stained.

A rough board table occupied the center of the room, and on it was a candle in a bowl, and a lantern. The coals in the fireplace were dead long since and his bunk was a tumbled pile of odorous blankets. Close beside him as he knelt by the window, was a wooden bucket. The wood was ingrained with white, and there was a milky film in the bottom. The water looked like skim milk. It was heavy with alkali. It was all he had.

Beside him on the floor, two boxes of shells were broken open. The floor around him was littered with empty shells, and the skin of his right hand was broken by a furrow, raw and bleeding, where a bullet had cut across the back of it.

He squinted his eyes at the desert sun and rolled his quid of chewing in his jaws. Then he spat. No head showed, no hand. Then a shot hit the stone wall near the window and whined away into the dancing heat.

He knew what they were waiting for. Eventually, he would have to sleep, but it was not that. They were waiting for the stage. By only a few minutes they had missed the last of yesterday's stages, and they had no intention of missing the one coming today. Wells believed there were only eight or ten Apaches out there now, but that was plenty. There wouldn't be more than three or four men on the stage, and they would be caught in the open.

From his window he could cover the front approaches to the stone barn beyond the corrals. The horses were in the barn, hence they were reasonably secure. The Indians had rushed him just as he had put them away, and if they had dashed for the house instead of for him, he would have been headed off, killed, scalped and dying by now.

Shooting with his pistol, he had made a break for the house. One bullet made a flesh wound in his side, and he had dropped two Indians. One of them was only wounded, but Wells had finished him off as he crawled for shelter in the rocks.

It was hot and stuffy in the closed-up stage station. Sweat trickled down his face and down his body under the sagging shirt. There was no time after daybreak that Alkali Basin could be described as cool.

Wells was nearing forty and looked all of fifty when unshaven. None of his years had been easy or comfortable. He had punched cows, driven a stage, placer mined. Nobody had ever called him a pleasant man, and when he smiled, which was rare, his parted lips revealed yellowed and broken teeth. His eyes were black and hard, implacable as the eyes of the Apaches he faced across that seventy yards of alkali and sand.

No one had ever known his real name. When asked, he merely said he came from Wells, so they called him that, and it served its purpose. The Apaches hated, feared, and respected him. They were not concerned about his name.

In the two months of his stay at Alkali Basin, they had attacked him five times. Nine Apaches died in those five attacks. To an Apache, who is supple as a rattler and hard to hit as a hell diver, that meant the stage tender was a warrior of the first order. Several more had been wounded, and two of their ponies killed. It now was a matter of honor that he die.

Wells put a finger in the water bucket and passed it over his cracked lips. He thought he glimpsed a toe against the white of the alkali behind the end of the wall. Taking careful aim, he squeezed off a shot. A startled yell rewarded him, then a hail of bullets. The storm died as soon as it began.

He crawled to the table and picked up a chunk of dried beef and cut off a piece. Putting it in his jaws, he went back to the window.

His battered hat lay on the floor. A pair of boots, whitened with alkali, stood in a corner under a stringy yellow slicker. On an extra chair was a cracked enamel washbasin containing some bloody water, a day old.

An hour passed slowly. He stared at the rocks in front of the house. They offered the only shelter available to more than one man at a time within a quarter of a mile. From the sides and back, there was no covered approach as the open alkali plain stretched off as far as the eye could reach in all directions. From the station, a slow rise of ground concealed the hills, miles away.

Almost a mile in front of the stage station lay a series of rocky ridges—foothills of the higher mountains beyond. A tongue of scattered rocks offered occasional concealment to a point some distance in front of the station. From there, to get within killing range, the Apaches had to dodge from rock to rock to get behind the low, natural wall in front of the station. Once there nothing could prevent them from lying entrenched for days and maintaining a sporadic fire on the station.

Water was no problem for them. Among the ridges, less than a mile off, was a good spring of only slightly brackish water. It was much better than that offered by the dug well at the station. Wells had killed one Indian going for water, but they offered only a fleeting, flickering target, visible for no more than a moment.

Time was running out. He knew that when he looked at the water in the bucket—yet he knew there would still be water left when his time was up. That would be when the stage reached the station. If it pulled up between the Indians and himself, they could use the stage as cover from his fire to get closer, while firing on the stage.

They knew as well as he, that they had not much longer to wait. That made them careful. A little while longer and then the stage would come rolling up to them. He could, of course, fire a few shots to warn the stage, but it would be in the open and fairly close up before they could hear, unless the wind was right.

Warned, they might get away, but with spent horses, and in that heat, he doubted it. Whether they did or not, he was a gone gosling.

Suddenly, his bloodshot eyes squinted, and then slowly widened with expectant triumph. Several feet behind the rock wall was a lone, flat-faced boulder. Lifting his rifle, Wells took aim at the face of that rock, and fired.

He was rewarded by a startled yell, and he fired three times, as rapidly as he could squeeze off the shots. One Indian, struck by a ricocheting bullet, lunged to full height, emitting a shrill scream, and Wells triggered his rifle again, to make sure of that one.

The Indian toppled forward over the wall, then hastily was dragged from view.

Wells, chuckling, reloaded his rifle and fired again. An Indian lunged to his feet and raced for the shelter of the rocks toward the ridge, and Wells let him go, content to be rid of them. Then a second Indian left. Wells tried two more shots at the flat rock, then lay quiet, staring with his smarting, red-rimmed eyes at the long, white emptiness of the desert.

An hour dragged slowly by, an hour of unrelenting heat and the endless white glare. A buzzard swung in lazy circles, high overhead. Wells left the muzzle of his rifle leaning against the sill, and put his head against the wall near the window. He dozed, only coming out of it at intervals to stare toward the wall. They might be gone, and they might not. He knew Apaches.

Once he tried a swallow of the thick, alkali water, but it choked him and he was only more thirsty than before. He tried a shot at the rock, but drew no answering fire. Then, after an interval, another shot. Silence, silence and the heat.

It would soon be stage time. He was very sleepy. He leaned his head against the wall and his lids grew heavy. His head bobbed loosely on his neck. Then he slept.

An instant only. His subconscious jerked him awake, frightened at what might have happened. He fired again, three quick shots.

There was no sound, no movement.

He crawled across the floor and looked from the window facing east. Only the wheelmarks showed, the wheelmarks that reached to the crest of the low rise that obscured his eastern view of the long, alkali basin and the distant hills. He returned to his vantage point and tried another shot.

He would get out of this on the next stage after the one coming. She had been right, of course, those eighteen years ago when she picked Ed instead of him. Ed settled into a quiet, easy life, but as for himself, he had lived on, a hard, lonely life along the frontiers. He had the ranch, of course, a cozy little place, and pleasant, but memories of her always drove him away, even after eighteen years.

A long hour dragged away before he heard the stage. It came over the rise and swept down upon the station with its pursuing cloud of dust, then braked to a halt. Wells got to his feet and lounged to the door. His eyes threw a brief glance at the desert and the wall, then he walked out to the stage.

"Howdy, Jim! How was the trip?"

"Hot," Jim climbed down from the stage top. "Where's the hosses?"

"Been sort of busy," Wells said, "I'll get them."

While Jim unhooked the spent team he went down to the stone barn. More asleep than awake he threw the harness on the horses. Jim came down to help him.

"Got the old man aboard," he said. "Macomber."

"Wonder if I'll get that powder?"

"Blazes, no! Judson says all he talks about is cuttin' expenses!"

They led the horses back and noticed that Price Macomber and his niece were out of the stage. Judson was watching them, wearily. Some little thing about the girl's face looked familiar to Wells.

"Any fresh water, my man?" Macomber asked.

"No," Wells looked around, his eyes bloodshot and hard, "but there's the well."

The name was the same, of course. Wells looked at the girl again. Price Macomber was glaring at him.

"I'd think," Macomber replied testily, "you could at least have some water ready for the passengers!"

Wells looked around, glaring. Then he saw the girl. She was standing helplessly, staring at him. Perspiration had streaked the dust on her face. She was the first woman he had seen in two months.

He straightened from fastening a trace chain, staring at the girl. She paled a little, but watched him, wide-eyed and fascinated.

Macomber noticed his stare and was suddenly angry. "Here!" he demanded. "Get us some water!"

Wells turned his head and looked at Macomber. His black eyes were cold and ugly. "Get it yourself!" he said.

Molly moved away from them and looked off across the alkali. She heard her uncle talking, low-voiced, to Judson. She heard him say, "We'll discharge this man!"

Judson was protesting. "Macomber, don't do it. We can't get anybody else. They are all afraid of this station because of the Apaches!"

"Nonsense! No man is indispensable!"

Molly noticed something bright and gleaming lying on the ground near a bundle of dusty hides and clothing. Curious, she started toward it. Then she stopped sharply, and her breath seemed to leave her. She felt as if she were going to faint. It was not a bunch of old hides and clothing, it was a dead man. A dead Indian.

"Uncle Price!" she cried. She turned and started on a stumbling run for the stage, her eyes great spots of darkness in her dead-white face.

"What's the matter?" Price Macomber wheeled about. "A snake?"

"No," she gasped, one hand on her heart, "it's a dead man! A dead—Indian!"

Price Macomber had heard about dead Indians, but he had never seen any kind of a dead man. He put one arm around his niece and stared at it, alarmed and fascinated.

Wells had not noticed. He was helping Jim carry bundles of food and ammunition into the stage station. When Jim put his armload down, he glanced around, noticing the bright brass of the empty shells. Mentally, he calculated, and then he looked up at Wells, his eyes respectful. "Trouble?" he asked.

"Yeah," Wells peeled the wrapping off a fresh plug of chewing. "Guess I got 'em all run off. I didn't have time to look. They hit me about noon, yesterday."

"That——?" Jim wet his dry lips with his tongue. With chill and unhappy realization he thought of what would have happened had the stage rolled up here with the Indians waiting. Him sitting up there on the box in plain sight, too.

They went outside. Macomber was helping his niece toward the stage. "What's up?" Jim asked, looking at them.

Judson glanced at Wells, seeing for the first time the mark of sleeplessness, the bullet-burned hand, the blood on his side. "You all right?" he demanded.

"Yeah," Wells replied shortly, "bring that powder?"

"No," Judson said, "Macomber says you don't need it."

Macomber was scarcely less shaken than his niece. He tried to avoid seeing the dead Indian. From here it was just a brown and patchy-looking hump on the alkali.

Wells walked over to him. "You get me some powder," he said flatly, "or get another man, and get that powder out here by the next stage!"

"See here!" Macomber's poise was shaken, but at this blow to the subject closest to his heart as well as to the respect he believed he deserved, his head came up. "Don't be talking to me like that! I don't see any reason for any powder out here. I told Judson that and I'll tell you now. We can't waste a lot of money on useless expenditure!"

Wells looked at him with hard, bitter eyes. "Those rocks out there," he gestured at the wall, "need blasting out."

He turned on his heels and started for the corral. Then he stopped on a sudden hunch and looked back. "Say," he said, "are you any relation to Edwin Macomber, of Denver?"

Price was startled. He turned around. "Why, I'm his brother! Why do you ask?"

Wells looked at him for a moment, and then he began to smile. Suddenly, he felt better. He walked on to the corral.

Price Macomber hesitated, staring after him, then he shrugged. Judson beside him, he walked to the wall. It was all nonsense, of course. This wall was completely out of the way, and no earthly excuse would warrant its blasting. He felt better, despite the smile on Wells' face, because this had proved his theory again, that most such unexplained items were the result of the impractical whims of impractical men.

He wanted the appearance of fairness, so he would at least look at the wall, but this was just another of the little details that proved how right he was in his theory. The dead Indian was not explained, but that could wait. He would ask about that when——

Price Macomber glanced across the wall and his face turned green. He backed away, retching violently. When he straightened, he dabbed at his lips with a handkerchief and stared at Judson, eyes bright with horror. There were three dead Indians beyond the wall. Each of them had been hit several times with jagged, ricocheting bullets.

Macomber stumbled a little as he hurried back toward the stage. This was an awful place! He must get out of here. Jim was on the box, holding the lines and waiting. Molly was talking to Wells, showing him something.

Price Macomber got hurriedly into the stage and sat down beside his niece. As they started to roll away, Judson waved to Wells. Macomber did not look back.

When they had gone a little way, he stiffened his face. "Send him that powder, Judson. The wall is an obstruction."

A thought occurred to him, and he turned to his niece. "What were you showing him? What did he say to you?"

She looked around. "I meant to tell you. He said he thought he knew my father and mother, so I showed him that picture of us. This one——"

Judson glanced at the picture as she handed it to her uncle, and could scarcely repress a smile. It was a picture of a prim-faced man who might have been Price Macomber himself. He wore spectacles and stood beside a very fat woman with two chins and a round, moonlike face. A face that once might have been quite pretty. Price Macomber nodded. His brother Ed, a solid, substantial man. He handed the picture back.

"What did he say when he saw the picture?"

She frowned, her eyes puzzled. "Why, he didn't say anything! He just stood there and laughed and laughed!"

His loaded rifle beside the door, the man called Wells began to sweep up the empty shells. "The ranch will look pretty good after this," he said aloud, "but after all, there are worse things than Apaches!"

MEN TO MATCH
THE HILLS

Cap Moffit was a careful man. That he was forty-two years old and still alive proved that beyond a doubt, for Cap Moffit was a professional killer.

He had learned the lesson of care from his first professional killing. In that case—and he had been fifteen years younger—Cap had picked a fight with his victim and shot him down and been nearly lynched as a result.

From that day on, Cap Moffit planned every killing as painstakingly as a great general might plan a battle. And he no longer made mistakes, knowing he need make but one. Over the years he had developed a technique, a carefully worked out pattern of operation.

He rode into the country over back trails, located the man he was to kill, and then spied upon him from cover until all his habits were known. Then, and only then, did Cap Moffit move in for the kill.

He always waited until his man was alone. He always caught him without cover in case the first shot was not a kill. He waited until his man was on the ground, so that a startled horse could not carry off a wounded man, or deliver the body too soon among friends. And also because it made that first shot more certain.

He never approached the body after a man fell, always went immediately away. And so far he had never failed.

Slightly below medium height, he was of slender build, and his face was narrow and quiet, with pale blue eyes and a tight, thin-lipped mouth. He invariably wore a narrow-brimmed gray hat, scuffed and solid, a gray vest over a blue cotton shirt, and faded jeans outside of boots with rundown heels. His gray coat was usually tied over his bedroll behind his saddle.

Cap Moffit lay comfortably on his stomach in a slight depression in the partial shade of the pines that crested Elk Ridge. Below him, in the long, green valley, was the T U Ranch, and living alone on that ranch was the man he was to kill. He was a man unknown to Moffit, although Cap knew his name was Jim Bostwick.

"Don't figure him for an easy one," his employer had warned. "The man's no gunfighter, but he gives the impression that he's been around. He's tough, and he won't scare at all. We tried that."

The advice bored Cap. It mattered not at all who or what Jim Bostwick was. He would have no chance to show himself as wise or tough. Once the situation was known, Cap Moffit would kill him, and that would be that. Of this, Cap Moffit had been sure.

Now, after five days of watching the ranch, he was no longer so positive. Men, he had discovered, were creatures of habit. All the little practices of living sooner or later fell into a pattern, and once that pattern was known, it was comparatively easy to find a point at which a man was usually motionless and within range.

For the first three days Jim Bostwick had come from the house at five-thirty in the morning and fed his horse a bait of oats and corn. He curried the horse while it finished the grain. Not many men took the time to care for a horse so thoroughly. That completed, he brought a wooden bucket from the house and, walking to the spring which was forty steps from the door, he filled the bucket and returned. Only then did he prepare breakfast.

By the second day Cap Moffit had decided that if the practice continued, the place for the killing was at the corral while Bostwick was currying the horse. The pole corral offered no cover, the man was practically motionless, and there was good cover for Moffit within forty yards. If the first shot failed there was time to empty the gun before Bostwick could reach shelter. And Cap Moffit had never missed once since he had entered his present profession. He did not dare miss.

Moreover, the spot he had selected for himself offered easy access and retreat over low ground, so he could not be seen reaching his objective. On the third day the pattern was repeated, and Cap Moffit decided if it held true one more day he would act.

He had taken every care to conceal his own presence. His camp was six miles away and carefully hidden. He never used the same vantage point on two successive days. He kept his fieldglasses shaded so their glass would not reflect light.

Yet, despite all his care, he had given himself away, and now the hunter was also the hunted.

On the morning of the fourth day, Jim Bostwick came from the house before Cap Moffit was settled into shooting position. Instead of going to the corral, he went around the house and disappeared from sight behind it. Puzzled by the sudden change Cap waited, sure the frame of habit would prove too strong and that the man would return to his usual ways. Suddenly, his eyes caught a movement at the corral and he was startled to see the horse eating from a bucket. Now, what the hell!

Jim Bostwick was nowhere in sight.

Then suddenly he appeared, coming from the spring with a bucket of fresh water. At the corner of the cabin he stopped and shaded his eyes, looking up the trail. Was he expecting visitors?

Bostwick disappeared within the house, and smoke began to

climb from the chimney. Cap Moffit lit a cigarette and tried to puzzle it out. If Bostwick followed his usual pattern now he would devote more than an hour to eating and cleaning up afterward. But why had he gone around the house? How had he reached the corral without being seen? And the spring? Could he possibly be aware that he was being watched?

Moffit dismissed that possibility. No chance of it, none at all. He had given no indication of his presence.

Nevertheless, men do not change a habit pattern lightly, and something had changed that of Bostwick, at least for a few minutes. And why had he looked so carefully up the trail? Was he expecting someone?

No matter. Moffit would kill Bostwick, and he would not wait much longer. Just to see if anyone did come.

Moffit was rubbing out his first cigarette of the day when his eye caught a flicker of movement. A big man, even bigger than Bostwick, was standing on the edge of the brush. He carried a rifle, and he moved toward the house. The fellow wore a buckskin shirt, had massive chest and shoulders, and walked with a curious, sidelong limp. At the door he suddenly ducked inside. Faintly, Moffit heard a rumble of voices, but he was too far away to hear anything that was said.

He scowled irritably. Who was the man in the buckskin shirt? What did *he* want?

Had he but known it, there was only one man in the cabin. That man was Bostwick himself. Stripping off the buckskin shirt, he removed the other shirts and padding he had worn under it and threw the worn-out hat to a hook. He was a big, tough man, to whom life had given much in trouble and hard work. He had come here to hold down this ranch for a friend until that friend could get back to make his own fight for it, a friend whose wife was fighting for her life now, and for the life of their child.

Jim Bostwick knew Charley Gore wanted this ranch and that he would stop at nothing to get it. They had tried to scare him first, but that hadn't worked. Gore had tried to ride him into a fight in town, when Gore was surrounded by his boys, and Bostwick had refused it. Knowing the game as he did, and knowing Gore, Bostwick had known this would not be the end of it.

Naturally wary, he had returned to the ranch, and days had gone by quietly. Yet he remained alert. And then one morning as he had started for the corral, he had caught a flash of something out of the corner of his eyes. He had not stopped nor turned his head, but when he was currying the horse he got a chance to study the rim of Elk Ridge without seeming to.

What he had seen was simple enough. A bird had started to light in a tree, then had flown up and away. Something was in that tree or was moving on the ground under it.

It could have been any one of many things.

Cap Moffit was a student of men and their habits. In the case of Jim Bostwick he had studied well, but not well enough. In the first place he had not guessed that Bostwick had a habit of suspicion, and that he also had a habit of liking to walk in the dark.

It was simply that he liked the cool of night, the stars, the stillness of it. He had walked at night after supper ever since he was a boy. And so it was that the night after the bird had flown up Jim Bostwick, wearing moccasins for comfort, took a walk. Only that night he went further afield.

He had been walking west of the ranch when he smelled dust. There was no mistaking it. He paused, listening, and heard the faint sound of hoofbeats dwindling away into distance.

At the point where he now stood was the junction between two little-used trails, and the hoofbeats had sounded heading south down the Snow Creek trail. But where could the rider have come from? The only place, other than the ranch, would be high on Elk Ridge itself.

Puzzled, Jim Bostwick made his way back to the ranch. If this rider had been on Elk Ridge that morning, and had caused that bird to fly up, he must have spent the day there. What was he doing there? Obviously he had been watching the ranch. Yet, Bostwick thought, he could have been mistaken about the bird. A snake or a mountain lion might have caused it to fly up. But he doubted it.

The following morning, an hour before day, he was not in the cabin. He was lying among the rocks above Snow Creek trail, several miles from the ranch, his horse hidden well back in the brush. He did not see the rider, for the man kept off the trail in the daylight, but he heard him. Heard him cough, heard his horse's hoofs strike stone, and knew from the sound that the rider had gone up through the trees to Elk Ridge.

When rider was safely out of the way, Jim Bostwick went out and studied the tracks. He then returned to the horse he had been riding and started back for the ranch, but he circled wide until he could ride down into the arroyo that skirted the north side of the ranch. This arroyo was narrow and invisible from the top of the ridge. In a grassy spot near the ranch house, he turned the horse into a small corral. It was where Tom Utterback kept his extra riding stock.

Then he crept back to the ranch house and went about his chores in the usual way, careful to indicate no interest in the ridge. He was also careful not to stand still where he would long be visible.

Inside the house, he prepared breakfast and considered the situation carefully. Obviously he was being watched. There was no point in watching him unless somebody meant to kill him. If the killer was that careful, he was obviously a dangerous man, and not to be taken lightly.

Why had he not made an attempt? Because he was stalking. Because he had not yet found the right opportunity.

Bostwick sat long over his coffee and mentally explored every approach to the situation. Putting himself in the unseen killer's place, he decided what he would do, and the following morning he began his puzzling tactics. Going around the house, he had gone down to the arroyo, then slipped back and, by using available cover, got the feed to his own horse. The ruse of the buckskin shirt had been used to make the watcher believe another man had entered the house. If he was correct in his guess that the killer was a careful man, the fellow would wait until he knew Bostwick was alone.

Bostwick was playing for time, working out a solution. Somehow he had to find out when the killer expected to kill, and from where. It was not long before he arrived at the same solution that had come to Cap Moffit.

The one time he could be depended upon to be at a given spot, not too far from cover, was when he curried his horse. That black was the love of his life, and he cared for the horse as he would for a child. The logical place was from the bed of the T U Creek. Flowing as it did, from Elk Ridge, it presented a natural approach. Searching it, Bostwick found a few faint tracks. The killer had been down this way, had made sure of his ground.

Jim Bostwick prepared supper that night with a scowl on his face. Something, some idea, nagged at his consciousness but was not quite realized. There was something he had missed, but one thing he was sure of. Whoever the killer was, he had been hired by Charley Gore.

Now it has been said that Jim Bostwick was no gunfighter. Yet there was a time when he had faced one, back in Yellowjacket, and Jim Bostwick had come out ahead. Those who knew him best knew that Jim Bostwick was a tough man, easy-going usually, but get him mad and he would walk into a den of grizzlies and drag the old man grizzly out by the scruff of his neck. He was that kind of man. Angered, he had an unreasoning courage that was absolutely without fear of consequences or death.

Jim Bostwick was growing angry now. He didn't like being hunted, and he liked even less the thought behind it, and the man behind it. More than once he had walked into the face of a gun, and with a queer kind of fatalism he was sure that some day he would die just that way. Yet he knew what he was going to do now. He was going to get this killer, and then he was going to get Charley Gore.

Yet he was not without the usual rough, ironic cowboy sense of humor so common in the west. The killer was up there on the hill hiding in the brush, and all the time the intended victim knew it. Suddenly, he began to chuckle. An idea had come to him, one he would enjoy.

Getting his pick and shovel he went out beside the house at a place just far enough away, but one which allowed no nearby cover, and commenced to dig. High on Elk Ridge, Cap Moffit stared down at Bostwick, puzzled by the digging. He became more puzzled as the hole became outlined. It was about six feet long and probably no more than half that wide. Jim Bostwick was digging a grave!

While digging, the idea that had been nagging at Bostwick's memory flowered suddenly. There had been other cases such as this. Lone men murdered without a clue, killed by some hidden marksman who then had vanished. There had been a family of three, slain one after another, over in the Panhandle.

Cap Moffit!

Jim Bostwick walked into the cabin and put the coffeepot on the stove. Nothing much was known about Cap Moffit. He was a rumor, perhaps a legend. A rancher had hinted once, at the beginning of a range war, that the proper way to end one was to send for Moffit. It had been a casual remark, yet it seemed to have information behind it. After that, there had been other stories, guarded, indefinite. It seemed that some of the more powerful cattlemen knew where they could get a killer when one was wanted.

Cap Moffit had been suspected of the Panhandle killings. His method had been talked about—the careful planning, the unerring marksmanship, the cold efficiency.

Now Jim Bostwick was sure the same man was lying up there on Elk Ridge. Of course, there were other killers for hire, but none with Moffit's careful, almost precise manner of killing. Realizing who he had to deal with sharpened his attention. If that was Cap Moffit, this was going to be anything but easy.

Cap had the reputation of shooting but once—and he did not miss.

Yet that in itself might be an advantage if Bostwick could continue to prevent him from getting the chance he wanted—or lead him into a trap, believing he had it.

He got a slab of wood and carved on it. Then he took it out

and placed it at the head of the open grave. From the top of the ridge, Moffit saw it. A cold, unimaginative man except when it came to killing, Cap Moffit was puzzled. Anything he did not understand disturbed him, and he did not understand this. For the first time he made a change in his plans. He decided to crawl close enough to read what was carved on the slab through his fieldglasses.

Bostwick came out, saddled up, always keeping the horse between himself and the available shelter. Then he mounted and rode away. Using the cut of the T U Creek, Cap Moffit came down the mountain and got into position under a huge old cottonwood and lifted his glass.

Cut deep and blackened with soot the words were plain, all too plain!

Here Lies
Cap Moffit, Killer
Shot Down
Upon
This Spot
April   1877

Cap Moffit lowered his glasses and wiped his eyes. He was crazy! It couldn't be! His second long look told the same story, and he lowered the glasses. He was known! Jim Bostwick knew him!

He looked again at the carved slab. An eerie feeling stole over him. It was unnatural. It was crazy. A man looking at his own grave marker. Only the date was blank, but the month was this month, the year this year. It was a warning—and it might be a prophecy.

Cap Moffit drew back and shook his head irritably. He was a fool to be disturbed by such a thing. Bostwick thought he was smart! Why, the fool! He'd show him!

Yet how had Bostwick known him? How could he be so sure?

Cap Moffit rolled a smoke and lit it, irritation strong within him, yet there was underlying worry, too. Had he known that at that very minute Jim Bostwick was scouting the ridge top, he would have been even more worried.

Jim Bostwick had gambled on Moffit's curiosity, and to some extent he did not care. There was a hard heedlessness about Jim Bostwick when aroused. He did not like being hunted. He did not like the necessity of being careful to avoid that assassin's bullet. Leaving the ranch, he had taken the trail toward town, but he had not followed it far; instead he had turned left and ridden round the end of Elk Ridge and mounted through the trees on the southern side.

Shortly, he had found Moffit's trail, knowing the tracks from those he had seen before. Now he rode with caution, his Winchester in his hand. Soon he found Moffit's horse, and on the inspiration of a moment, he stripped off saddle and bridle and turned the animal loose. Then he followed the trail of the walking man and found his various hideouts on the ridgetop.

Rightly, he deduced that the killer was down below, but he guessed wrong. Even as he found the last place where Moffit had rested under the big pine, Moffit was coming back up the gully of the T U Creek. He was coming slowly and carefully as was his wont, but his mind was preoccupied. He did not like the thought that his prospective victim knew who he was. What if he talked? What if, even now, he had gone to town to report to the sheriff?

Even as this thought struck him, Moffit noticed something else. He had reached the back slope of the ridge, and he noticed a black saddled horse standing some two hundred yards away. Yet even as he saw the horse, the black's head jerked up, its ears pricked, and it looked at him.

Something moved in the brush near the horse's head, and Cap Moffit's rifle came up, leaping to his shoulder. He saw the leaping body of Jim Bostwick, and he fired. The black sprang away, running, and Bostwick dropped, but as he hit ground, he fired!

The bullet clipped leaves not inches from his head, and Cap Moffit dropped to the ground. He slid downhill a few feet, then got up and, running lightly, circled toward his horse. He had no wish to fight a gun battle on that brush-covered, boulder-strewn mountainside. Such a battle would be too indefinite, for there not only marksmanship would be important, but wood-craft as well.

Moffit ran lightly toward his horse, then stopped. The horse was gone. An empty bridle and saddle awaited him!

Furious, he dropped back a few feet and took shelter among the rocks. He was fairly trapped! Unless—unless he could get Bostwick's horse.

It had run off, but would not go far. Probably his bullet had burned it. Yet he must be careful, for even now Bostwick might be coming down the mountain. The man would rightly deduce that the ambusher would head for his horse, so even now he might be drawing near.

Cap Moffit began to sweat. Something had gone wrong this time, and it would take all his ingenuity to get himself out of it alive. The man hunting him was no fool.

Jim Bostwick, warned by the quick swing of the black's head, had dropped. It was that dropping movement which drew the shot. Instantly, he rolled over and began to crawl, worming his way a full thirty yards before he stopped. His own bullet had been an instinctive reply, and he had no idea how close it had come. Yet there was nothing in him that warned him to retreat. His only idea was to get the killer for hire who had come here to kill him.

The woods were still, and the sun was hot. Here under the trees, now that the breeze had died, it was sticky and still. The air was sultry, and sweat trickled down his face. His neck itched from dust and from pine needles picked up when he rolled over. There was the acrid smell of gunpowder from his rifle, and the silence of the woods. His horse had stopped running somewhere off among the trees.

Jim Bostwick waited. Patience and alertness would win now. Here in the woods, anything might happen. His throat felt dry and he wished for a drink. Somewhere he thought he heard a faint sound, but he did not move. He was lying on brown, parched pine needles in the blazing hot sun. Around him were the sharp edges and corners of rock thrust from the earth of the ridge, and not far away were larger boulders and a huge fallen log. It offered better cover, but more suspicious cover than he now had.

He waited. Somewhere an eagle cried. Something tiny scurried among the leaves. Then all was still.

His horse would come back to him. The black was trained to do just that. Yet even as he realized the black would soon be coming, another thought occurred. Cap Moffit would try to catch the horse and get away! Or kill him!

Moffit was cunning. Suppose he realized the horse was going back to Bostwick? And that he had only to wait and be guided by the horse? The black would find him, for a horse can smell out a trail as well as some dogs, if the trail is not an old one. More than once Jim Bostwick had seen horses do just that, and the black had often followed him in that way.

The sun was blazing hot. There was no breeze. The rocks glistened with desert varnish, smooth as mirrors. Far away he heard the horse walking. Bostwick did not like waiting. It had not been his way to wait, but to barge right in, swinging or shooting, and letting things happen as they would. This was Cap Moffit's game. The cool, careful killer's game.

Moffit would be coming. Moffit *had* to kill him now. He forced himself to lie still. The black was nearer now. Somewhere he heard a faint whisper of sound, the brushing of jeans on a rock or branch. He slid his hand back to the trigger guard of the rifle, gripped the gun with two hands, ready to leap and shoot.

There was no further sound. The horse had stopped. Probably the black had seen Moffit.

Bostwick waited, sweating, his back cooking under the direct rays of the spring sun. Every muscle was tensed and ready for action. Suddenly there was a flashing movement and a gun blasted, a rifle bullet cut through his hat brim and burned along his back. Instantly he fired, not holding his shots, one in the center, then quickly left and right of the spot from which the shot had come.

Another bullet notched his ear and he rolled over, down the south side of the ridge, trying to avoid the next shot until he could get to his feet. A bullet smashed dirt into his eyes and he fired blindly.

Rolling over, he lunged to his feet and dived for the shelter of some rocks. A bullet smashed into the rocks and ricocheted almost in his face, whining past his ear with a scream like a banshee. He hit ground and behind him he heard Moffit running to get another shot. The rifle roared behind him and he felt his rifle smashed from his hands and saw its stock was splintered.

He lunged to his feet again and threw himself in a long dive for some brush as the rifle bellowed again. He felt the shock of that bullet and knew that he was hit. Moffit wasn't stopping, but was coming on. Bostwick whirled and grabbed for his six-shooter.

As it came into his hand, he threw himself to his feet just as Moffit sprang into the open. Jim Bostwick braced himself with the world rolling under him and the sweat in his eyes and the smell of blood in his nostrils, and he threw lead from his .44 and saw dust jump from Moffit's shirt. The smaller man fell back and hit the ground, but shot from the ground. Jim Bostwick felt the shock of that bullet, but he fired as he was falling, and missed.

He rolled over into the brush and, filled with sudden panic that he might get caught there in the open, he fought and scrambled his way through the brush. Fighting to get to shelter, he left a trail of scratched earth and blood behind him.

When he could stop, he rolled over to a sitting position and reloaded his six-shooter. There was no sound. He knew that Cap Moffit was not dead, but that one of them would die here, perhaps both. His gun loaded, he looked to his wounds. He had a hole through the fleshy upper part of his thigh, and it was bleeding badly. He plugged that with a handkerchief, torn to use on both sides, then examined his chest.

He was afraid the bullet had struck him in a vital spot, for the shock of it had turned him sick. However, he was fortunate. The bullet had struck his hip bone and ricocheted off, making a nasty open wound, but nothing deep. He drew the lips of the wound together and bound it with his torn shirt.

There was neither sound nor movement. His canteen was on his horse, and the horse would come if he called. The black was probably waiting for just that.

Jim Bostwick checked his belt. His six-shooter now held six shells, for he was going to be using it, not carrying it, and there were still twenty-odd shells in his belt. If he could not win with that number, he would never win.

Rage welled up in him and suddenly, heedless of consequences, he shouted, "I'm going to kill you, Cap! You've drygulched your last man!"

"Come and get me then!" Moffit taunted. "You're so full of holes now you won't last the night!"

Jim Bostwick rubbed his unshaven jaw. He rolled over, thrusting his six-shooter in his belt. His arms were strong and unhurt, he could drag himself, or hobble if he could get up on his good leg.

Slowly and painfully, he worked his way along the side of the ridge into the deeper brush and trees. Dust and sweat caked his face, but his heavy jaw was set and frozen against the biting pain. In a dense clump of brush, he waited. The horse was his ace-in-the-hole. The black would not leave, and he could call to him. Had Moffit been active, he might have reached the horse, but smelling of blood, there was small chance of any stranger getting near.

Under the bushes, Bostwick lowered himself and lay on the pine needles, panting hoarsely. He must not pass out—he must stay alert. Cap Moffit had not only money for a reason now, but he must kill Bostwick or die himself.

Pain welled up and went through the rancher. He gritted his teeth against it, and against the weakness that was in him. Soon he would start out. He would get going.

A faint coolness touched his face, a stirring breath of air. He lifted his head and looked around. There was a bank of clouds over the mountains, piled-up thunderheads. The coolness touched his face again, breeze with the smell of rain in it. The country could use rain. The grass needed it. His head sank forward.

Only a minute it seemed, yet when he opened his eyes it was black—black and wet. It was raining. He had passed out.

His eyes had opened to darkness and a vast roaring that filled the world, a roaring of gigantic masses of wind and almost continuous thunder. Like a solid wall the wind swept the ridge, bending the huge trees like willows and sweeping the rocks with icy scythes of driving rain, pounding the earth and lashing at his cowering, rain-drenched body.

Suddenly, below the awful roar of the wind along the towering ridge, he heard another sound—faint, but definite. A vast bursting flare of lightning illumined the ridge with blinding incandescent light. Through the flare there was a vicious whiplash of vivid blue flame, and his brain seemed split apart by a rending crash!

The huge pine near which he had been lying seemed to burst under his eyes and the towering mass of the tree toppled, falling away from him, leaving the dead-white fractured center exposed to the rain and the wind. Lightning whipped at the ridge, and the earth and rocks smelled of brimstone and charred pine needles.

And below the roar he heard again that whisper of sound. Lightning flared, and in the white glare he saw Cap Moffit, eyes wide and staring, Cap Moffit, poised and waiting for the flare, gun in hand. Even as he glimpsed him, Moffit fired!

The bullet missed, and Jim Bostwick rolled over, grabbing wildly, desperately, for his own gun. Wildly he fired, hurling three fast shots at the place from which the shot had come. With a lunge he made it to his feet, shot out a hand and grabbed the lightning-blasted stump even as lightning flared again. They shot as one man, then Bostwick let go his hold and lunged through the driving wall of rain at the spot where he had seen Moffit. They came together, and Bostwick struck wickedly with his gunbarrel and missed, falling forward. He rolled over quickly and saw the dark figure swaying above him.

Moffit fired, the blast of flame only feet from Bostwick's face. He felt the wicked sting of burning powder and felt the blow of the bullet as it struck him.

Huge billowing clouds rolled low over the ridge, and the whiplike flashes of lightning danced like dervishes of flame along the ridge. The forest would have been aflame had it not been for the great masses of water that were driven along it.

Moffit fired again, but he was weaving like one of the bushes around them and the shot missed. Bostwick rolled over. Grimly he struggled, moaning with eagerness to get up, to get his hands on Moffit. He swung out a wild, clutching hand and grabbed one of the killer's ankles. He jerked and the man fell and, bloody and wounded as Bostwick was, he clawed to grab a hold on the man's throat. There was another vivid streak of lightning, then Moffit's gun roared. . . .

Consciousness returned, but slowly. Jim Bostwick lay flat on his face on the rocks of the ridge, swept bare by the violence of wind and rain. Around him, where all had been rushing wind and roaring rain, there was dead stillness. His head thudded with hammer-blows of agony. His shoulder and arm were stiff, one leg seemed useless, and every movement seared him with pain.

The rain had ceased. The wind had gone. The might of the thunder in the lonely ravines to the south and west had turned to the far-off mumbling of a puppy. Storm-tossed clouds scattered the skies and vied with the stars for attention. And Jim Bostwick lay sprawled and alone on the ridge, his body spent, weakened from loss of blood and the whipping rain. And then he put out a hand and found his gun. Somehow he got his knees under him and lifted himself. He spun the cylinder of the gun and it turned.

Fumbling with clumsy fingers, he worked the ejector rod and pushed out the empty shells. Then he loaded the gun with care from his belt. There was nobody near him. He could see that. Wherever Moffit was, he was not here.

Jim Bostwick fumbled around, feeling, then he found a broken limb. Using it for a crutch, he got to his feet.

Blackie would have gone. The storm would have driven him off. Bostwick knew that straight ahead of him and more than a thousand feet down was the ranch, and if he was to live, he must get back to that ranch.

It was no use to try going around by the trail. He would never make it. Somehow he must fumble and fall and feel his way to the bottom. How long it took him, he did not know, but he knew when he reached it, and his fingers found something else. A horse's track!

If a track was here, it had to be made since the storm. He called out, risking a shot from Moffit, if he was still alive and nearby. He called again, and again. Then he heard a low whinny and the *clop, clop* of hoofs.

"Blackie!" he whispered. "Blackie!"

The horse snorted and shied, then came nearer, snuffling in the darkness. He reached up, and the horse shied again. He spoke his name and Blackie stood still. One hand got the stirrup, and then he pulled himself into the wet saddle.

"Home, Blackie!" he whispered and, as if waiting for just that, the black turned and started out across the little valley toward the house.

Sagging over the pommel, he still managed to cling to it, and when the black stopped at the steps of the house, he almost fell from the saddle. And when he hit the steps his hand struck the face. He grabbed for a gun, then stopped. The face was still, the body unmoving, but warm.

In the still, cold light from a vague gray predawn, he stared down at the crumpled figure. It was Cap Moffit.

Jim Bostwick chuckled, a hoarse, choking sound. "You—you couldn't take it!" he sneered.

Turning over, he reached with his good hand for the girth and managed to get it loose and let the saddle fall. Then he pulled the black's head down and got the bridle off.

"Take a roll, boy," he whispered, "and rustle some grub."

He got the door open, then got a hand on Moffit's collar and dragged him inside, leaving one boot caught on the step with a spur. He got Moffit's gun and put them both near his hand.

It took him an hour to get his wounds uncovered, and another hour to get them bathed and dressed, after a fashion. As he worked, he looked grimly at the unconscious man. "I'm still moving," he said, "I'm going to come through."

When he had his wounds dressed, he went to work on Moffit. He was working on nerve, he knew that, and nothing but nerve. He kept himself going, forced himself to keep moving. He got the wounded man fixed up and got water heating on the stove, then slumped in a chair, his face haggard and bearded, his eyes hollow, his hair tangled with mud and blood—the last bullet had cut his scalp open and given him what was probably a mild concussion. He stared across at the unconscious killer, his eyes bleak.

When the water was hot, he made coffee and laced it with whisky and burned his mouth gulping a cup of it, then another. Then he pulled himself, sliding the chair by gripping the wall, until he was close to Cap Moffit. He tied the wounded killer's wrists and ankles. Some time later, sprawled on the bed, he passed out again.

Hours later, with daylight streaming in the door from a sinking sun, he awakened. His eyes went at once to Moffit. The wounded man lay on the floor, glaring at him.

Bostwick swung his feet to the floor and stared blearily at Moffit. "Trussed up like a dressed chicken!" he sneered. "A hell of a gunman you are!"

Moffit stared at him. "You don't look so good yourself!" he retorted.

Bostwick caught the ledge along the wall with his good hand and pulled himself erect. He slapped the gun in his waistband. "I still got a gun," he said, and crept along the wall to the kitchen where he got the fire going, then fell into a chair. "You ain't so hot with a short gun," he said.

"I got *you*."

Bostwick chuckled. "Yeah, you're holding me, ain't you? I'm dead, ain't I? You two-bit imitation of a killer, you never saw the day you could kill me."

Moffit shook his head. "Maybe you're right," he said. "You must have three bullets in you now."

"Four hits you made." Bostwick chuckled. "I'm carrying no lead."

His stomach felt sick, but he managed to get water on the stove and make coffee. When he fell back in the chair again he felt weak and sicker.

"You better set still," Moffit said. "You're all in." He paused. "Whyn't you shoot me when you had the chance?"

"Aw—" Bostwick stared at him, grim humor in his eyes—"I like a tough man. I like a fighter. You did pretty good up on that mountain last night, pretty good for a drygulching killer."

Cap Moffit said nothing. For the first time the words of another man hurt. He stared down at his sock feet, and he had no reply to make.

"You going to turn me in for a hanging?" he finally asked.

"Naw," Bostwick poured coffee into a cup and slid it across the table. "Somebody'll shoot you sure as the Lord made little apples. You ever come back around here and I will. This here Tom Utterback who owns this spread, he's a good man."

"He's got a good man for a friend."

Two sick, wounded men struggled through four days, and it was Bostwick who struggled. Moffit watched him, unbelieving. It was impossible that any man could be so tenacious of life, so unbelievably tough. Yet this big, hard man was not giving up. No man, Moffit felt suddenly, could kill such a man. There was something in him, something black, bitter and strong, something that would not die.

On the sixth morning, Cap Moffit was gone. He had taken a gray from the other corral and he had gone off, riding his recovered saddle—wounded, but alive.

Tom Utterback rode up to the ranch on the ninth day. He

stared at the pale shadow of a man who greeted him, gun in hand. He stared at the bloody bandage on the leg.

"You wasn't in that gunfight in town, was you?" he demanded.

"What gunfight?"

"Stranger name of Cap Moffit. He had some words with Charley Gore and two of his boys. They shot it out."

"They get him?"

"Don't know. He was shot up bad, but he rode out on his own horse."

"What happened to Gore?"

Utterback shook his head. "That stranger was hell on wheels. He killed Gore and one of his men and wounded the other."

"Yeah, he was a good man, all right." Jim Bostwick backed up and sat down in a chair. "Make some coffee, will you? And a decent meal. I'm all in."

A few minutes later he opened his eyes. He looked up at the ceiling, then out the door where another sun was setting.

"I'm glad he got away," he muttered.

THE DEFENSE OF SENTINEL

When the morning came, Finn McGraw awakened into a silent world. His eyes opened to the wide and wondering sky where a solitary cloud wandered reluctantly across the endless blue.

At first he did not notice the silence. He had awakened, his mouth tasted like a rain-soaked cathide, he wanted a drink, and he needed a shave. This was not an unusual situation.

He heaved himself to a sitting position, yawned widely, scratching his ribs—and became aware of the silence.

No sound . . . No movement. No rattling of well buckets, no cackling of hens, no slamming of doors. Sentinel was a town of silence.

Slowly, his mind filling with wonder, Finn McGraw climbed to his feet. With fifty wasted years behind him, he had believed the world held no more surprises. But Sentinel was empty.

Sentinel, where for six months Finn McGraw had held the unenvied position of official town drunk. He had been the tramp, the vagabond, the useless, the dirty, dusty, unshaven, whisky-sodden drunk. He slept in alleys. He slept in barns— wherever he happened to be when he passed out.

Finn McGraw was a man without a home. Without a job. Without a dime. And now he was a man without a town.

What can be more pitiful than a townless town drunk?

Carefully, McGraw got to his feet. The world tipped edge-wise and he balanced delicately and managed to maintain his equilibrium. Negotiating the placing of his feet with extreme caution, he succeeded in crossing the wash and stumbling up the bank on the town side. Again, more apprehensively, he listened.

Silence.

No smoke rising from chimneys, no barking dogs, no horses. The street lay empty before him, like a street in a town of ghosts.

Finn McGraw paused and stared at the phenomenon. Had he, like Rip van Winkle, slept for twenty years?

Yet he hesitated, for well he knew the extreme lengths that Western men would go for a good practical joke. The thought came as a relief. That was it, of course, this was a joke. They had all gotten together to play a joke on him.

His footsteps echoed hollowly on the boardwalk. Tentatively, he tried the door of the saloon. It gave inward, and he pushed by the inner, batwing doors and looked around. The odor of stale whisky mingled with cigar smoke lingered, lonesomely, in the air. Poker chips and cards were scattered on the table, but there was nobody. . . . Nobody at all!

The back bar was lined with bottles. His face brightened. Whisky! Good whisky, and his for the taking! At least, if they had deserted him they had left the whisky behind.

Caution intervened. He walked to the back office and pushed open the door. It creaked on a rusty hinge and gave inward, to emptiness.

"Hey?" His voice found only an echo for company. "Where is everybody?"

No answer. He walked to the door and looked out upon the

street. Suddenly the desire for human companionship blossomed into a vast yearning.

He rushed outside. He shouted. His voice rang emptily in the street against the false-fronted buildings. Wildly, he rushed from door to door. The blacksmith shop, the livery stable, the saddle shop, the bootmaker, the general store, the jail—all were empty, deserted.

He was alone.

Alone! What had *happened*? Where *was* everybody? Saloons full of whisky, stores filled with food, blankets, clothing. All these things had been left unguarded.

Half-frightened, Finn McGraw made his way to the restaurant. Everything there was as it had been left. A meal half-eaten on the table, dishes unwashed. But the stove was cold.

Aware suddenly of a need for strength that whisky could not provide, Finn McGraw kindled a fire in the stove. From a huge ham he cut several thick slices. He went out back and rummaged through the nests and found a few scattered eggs. He carried these inside and prepared a meal.

With a good breakfast under his belt, he refilled his coffee cup and rummaged around until he found a box of cigars. He struck a match and lighted a good Havana, pocketing several more. Then he leaned back and began to consider the situation.

Despite the excellent meal and the cigar, he was uneasy. The heavy silence worried him, and he got up and went cautiously to the door. Suppose there was something here, something malign and evil? Suppose— Angrily, he pushed the door open. He was going to stop supposing. For the first time in his life he had a town full of everything, and he was going to make the most of it.

Sauntering carelessly down the empty street to the Elite General Store, he entered and coolly began examining the clothing. He found a hand-me-down gray suit and changed his clothes. He selected new boots and donned them as well as a white cambric shirt, a black string tie, and a new black hat. He pocketed a fine linen handkerchief. Next he lighted another cigar, spat into the brass spittoon, and looked upon life with favor.

On his right as he turned to leave the store was a long rack of rifles, shotguns and pistols. Thoughtfully, he studied them. In his day—that was thirty years or so ago—he had been a sharpshooter in the Army.

He got down a Winchester '73, an excellent weapon, and loaded it with seventeen bullets. He appropriated a fine pair of Colts, loaded them, and belted them on, filling the loops with cartridges. Taking down a shotgun, he loaded both barrels with buckshot, then he sauntered down to the saloon, rummaged under the bar until he came up with Dennis Magoon's excellent Irish whisky, and poured three fingers into a glass.

Admiring the brown, beautiful color, the somber amber, as he liked to call it, he studied the sunlight through the glass, then tasted it.

Ah! Now that was something like it! There was a taste of bog in that! He tossed off his drink, then refilled his glass.

The town was his—the whole town—full of whisky, food, clothing—almost everything a man could want.

But *why*? Where *was* everybody?

Thoughtfully, he walked outside. The silence held sway. A lonely dust devil danced on the prairie outside of town, and the sun was warm.

At the edge of town he looked out over the prairie toward the mountains. Nothing met his eye save a vast, unbelievable stretch of grassy plain. His eyes dropped to the dust and with a kind of shock he remembered that he could read sign. Here were the tracks of a half-dozen rigs, buckboards, wagons and carts. From the horse tracks all were headed the same direction—east.

He scowled and, turning thoughtfully, he walked back to the livery barn.

Not a horse remained. Bits of harness were dropped on the ground—a spare saddle. Everything showed evidence of a sudden and hasty departure.

An hour later, having made the rounds, Finn McGraw returned to the saloon. He poured another glass of the Irish, lighted another Havana, but now he had a problem.

The people of the town had not vanished into thin air, they had made a sudden, frightened, panic-stricken rush to get away from the place.

That implied there was, in the town itself, some evil.

Finn McGraw tasted the whisky and looked over his shoulder uncomfortably. He tiptoed to the door, looked one way, then suddenly the other way.

Nothing unusual met his gaze.

He tasted his whisky again and then, crawling from the dusty and cobwebbed convolutions of his brain, long befuddled by alcohol, came realization.

Indians!

He remembered some talk the night before while he was trying to bum a drink. The Ladder Five ranch had been raided and the hands had been murdered. Victorio was on the warpath, burning, killing, maiming. *Apaches!*

The Fort was east of here! Some message must have come, some word, and the inhabitants had fled like sheep and left him behind.

Like a breath of icy air he realized that he was alone in the town, there was no means of escape, no place to hide. And the Apaches were coming!

Thrusting the bottle of Irish into his pocket, Finn McGraw made a break for the door. Outside, he rushed down to the Elite General Store. This building was of stone, low and squat, and built for defense, as it had been a trading post and stage station before the town grew up around it. Hastily, he took stock.

Moving flour barrels, he rolled them to the door to block it. Atop the barrels he placed sacks, bales and boxes. He barred the heavy back door, then blocked the windows. In the center of the floor he built a circular parapet of more sacks and barrels for a last defense. He got down an armful of shotguns and proceeded to load ten of them. These he scattered around at various loopholes, with a stack of shells by each.

Then he loaded several rifles. Three Spencer .56's, a Sharps .50 and seven Winchester '73's.

He loaded a dozen of the Colts and opened boxes of ammunition. Then he lighted another Havana and settled down to wait.

The morning was well nigh gone. There was food enough in the store, and the position was a commanding one. The store was thrust out from the line of buildings in such a way that it commanded the approaches of the street in both directions, yet it was long enough so that he could command the rear of the buildings as well, by running to the back.

The more he studied his position the more he wondered why Sentinel inhabitants had left the town undefended. Only blind, unreasoning panic could have caused such a flight.

At noon he prepared himself a meal from what he found in the store, and waited. It was shortly after high sun when the Indians came.

The Apaches might have been scouting the place for hours; Finn had not seen them. Now they came cautiously down the street, creeping hesitantly along.

From a window that commanded the street, old Finn McGraw waited. On the windowsill he had four shotguns, each with two barrels loaded with buckshot. And he waited . . .

The Apaches, suspecting a trap, approached cautiously. They peered into empty buildings, flattened their faces against windows, then came on. The looting would follow later. Now the Indians were suspicious, anxious to know if the town was deserted. They crept forward.

Six of them bunched to talk some forty yards away. Beyond them a half dozen more Apaches were scattered in the next twenty yards. Sighting two of his shotguns, Finn McGraw rested a hand on each. The guns were carefully held in place by sacks weighting them down, and he was ready. He squeezed all four triggers at once!

The concussion was terrific! With a frightful roar, the four barrels blasted death into the little groups of Indians, and instantly, McGraw sprang to the next two guns, swung one of them slightly, and fired again.

Then he grabbed up a heavy Spencer and began firing as fast as he could aim, getting off four shots before the street was empty. Empty, but for the dead.

Five Apaches lay stretched in the street. Another, dragging himself with his hands, was attempting to escape.

McGraw lunged to his feet and raced to the back of the building. He caught a glimpse of an Indian and snapped a quick shot. The Apache dropped, stumbled to his feet, then fell again and lay still.

That was the beginning. All through the long, hot afternoon the battle waged. Finn McGraw drank whisky and swore. He loaded and reloaded his battery of guns. The air in the store was stifling. The heat increased, the store smells thickened, and over it all hung the acrid smell of gunpowder.

Apaches came to recover their dead and died beside them. Two naked warriors tried to cross the rooftops to his building, and he dropped them both. One lay on the blistering roof, the other rolled off and fell heavily.

Sweat trickled into McGraw's eyes, and his face became swollen from the kick of the guns. From the front of the store he could watch three ways, and a glance down the length of the store allowed him to see a very limited range outside. Occasionally he took a shot from the back window, hoping to keep them guessing.

Night came at last, bringing a blessed coolness, and old Finn McGraw relaxed and put aside his guns.

Who can say that he knows the soul of the Indian? Who can say what dark superstitions churn inside his skull? For no Apache will fight at night, since he believes the souls of men killed in darkness must forever wander, homeless and alone. Was it fear that prevented an attack now? Or was it some fear of this strange, many-weaponed man—if man he was—who occupied the dark stone building?

And who can say with what strange expressions they stared

at each other as they heard from their fires outside the town the weird thunder of the old piano in the saloon, and the old man's whisky-bass rolling out the words of "The Wearing of the Green"; "Drill, Ye Tarriers, Drill"; "Come Where My Love Lies Dreaming" and "Shenandoah."

Day came and found Finn McGraw in the store, ready for battle. The old lust for battle that is the birthright of the Irish had risen within him. Never, from the moment he realized that he was alone in a town about to be raided by Apaches, had he given himself a chance for survival. Yet it was the way of the Irish to fight, and the way even of old, whisky-soaked Finn.

An hour after dawn, a bullet struck him in the side. He spun half-around, fell against the flour barrels and slid to the floor. Blood flowed from the slash, and he caught up a handful of flour and slapped it against the wound. Promptly he fired a shot from the door, an aimless shot, to let them know he was still there. Then he bandaged his wound.

It was a flesh wound, and would have bled badly but for the flour. Sweat trickled into his eyes, grime and powder smoke streaked his face. But he moved and moved again, and his shotguns and rifles stopped every attempt to approach the building. Even looting was at a minimum, for he controlled most of the entrances, and the Apaches soon found they must dispose of their enemy before they could profit from the town.

Sometime in the afternoon, a bullet knocked him out, cutting a furrow in his scalp, and it was nearing dusk when his eyes opened. His head throbbed with enormous pain, his mouth was dry. He rolled to a sitting position and took a long pull at the Irish, feeling for a shotgun. An Apache was even then fumbling at the door.

He steadied the gun against the corner of a box. His eyes blinked. He squeezed off both barrels and, hit in the belly, the Apache staggered back.

At high noon on the fourth day, Major Magruder with a troop of cavalry, rode into the streets of Sentinel. Behind him were sixty men of the town, all armed with rifles.

At the edge of town, Major Magruder lifted a hand. Jake Carter and Dennis Magoon moved up beside him. "I thought you said the town was deserted?"

His extended finger indicated a dead Apache.

Their horses walked slowly forward. Another Apache sprawled there dead . . . and then they found another.

Before the store four Apaches lay in a tight cluster, another savage was stretched at the side of the walk. Windows of the store were shattered and broken, a great hole had been blasted in the door. At the Major's order, the troops scattered to search the town. Magruder swung down before the store.

"I'd take an oath nobody was left behind," Carter said.

Magruder shoved open the store. The floor inside was littered with blackened cartridge cases and strewn with empty bottles. "No one man could fire that many shells or drink that much whisky," Magruder said positively.

He stooped, looking at the floor and some flour on the floor. "Blood," he said.

In the saloon they found another empty bottle and an empty box of cigars.

Magoon stared dismally at the empty bottle. He had been keeping count, and all but three of the bottles of his best Irish glory was gone. "Whoever it was," he said sorrowfully, "drank up some of the best whisky ever brewed."

Carter looked at the piano. Suddenly he grabbed Magoon's arm. "McGraw!" he yelled. " 'Twas Finn McGraw!"

They looked at each other. It couldn't be! And yet—who had seen him? Where was he now?

"Who," Magruder asked, "is McGraw?"

They explained, and the search continued. Bullets had clipped the corners of buildings, bullets had smashed water barrels along the street. Windows were broken, and there were nineteen dead Indians—but no sign of McGraw.

Then a soldier yelled from outside of town, and they went that way and gathered around. Under the edge of a mesquite bush, a shotgun beside him, his new suit torn and bloodstained, they found Finn McGraw.

Beside him lay two empty bottles of the Irish. Another,

partly gone, lay near his hand. A rifle was propped in the forks of the bush, and a pistol had fallen from his holster. There was blood on his side and blood on his head and face.

"Dead!" Carter said. "But what a battle!"

Magruder bent over the old man, then he looked up, a faint twinkle breaking the gravity of his face. "Dead, all right," he said. "Dead *drunk!*"